'SEES'

When Barbara Willard moved to Ashdown Forest more than thirty years ago, she thought it a deserted and mysterious place. But as time passed and her sense of the people who had lived there centuries before grew stronger and stronger, she changed her mind. This sense of the past began to find its way into her writing too. "My stories," she says, "are not 'historical novels' in the grand sense – I am no scholar – but they might be called an attempt at putting on old clothes and seeing what they feel like. I can't help getting very involved in my characters' lives."

She found writing *The Queen of the Pharisees' Children* an especially poignant experience. "I had written about kings, queens, barons, knights and the rest – now I wanted to tell the tale of people who had nothing. I began writing it in autumn and the troubles of Moll and Sim and the rest became my troubles as the wind grew chill and the forest trees cast off their sheltering leaves..."

One of the most distinguished of all British writers for children, Barbara Willard has written over forty books, including the *Mantlemass* books, one of which, *The Iron Lily*, won the Guardian Award in 1974. *The Queen of the Pharisees' Children* won the 1984 Whitbread Award. She lives in a cottage on the edge of Ashdown Forest and is an ardent conservationist.

Also by Barbara Willard

THE MANTLEMASS BOOKS
The Lark and the Laurel
The Sprig of Broom
A Cold Wind Blowing
The Eldest Son
The Iron Lily
A Flight of Swans
Harrow and Harvest
The Keys of Mantlemass
The Miller's Boy

Ned Only

THE QUEEN OF THE PHARISEES' CHILDREN

BARBARA WILLARD

WALKER BOOKS
LONDON

First published 1983 by Julia MacRae Books
This edition published 1989 by Walker Books Ltd
87 Vauxhall Walk, London SE11 5HJ

Printed in Great Britain by Cox and Wyman Ltd, Reading

British Library Cataloguing in Publication Data
Willard, Barbara
The queen of the pharisees' children.
I. Title
823'.914[J]   PZ7
ISBN 0-7445-1310-3

1

ALL that spring was fine and warm and the summer that followed made living easy. Then it was past mid-summer and on to harvest, and still good fortune held firm. The moon that rose over a contented countryside seemed to Will the biggest he had seen in almost thirteen years. The colour of ripe quince as it climbed up from the horizon, it shed so warm and full a light that any shadows seemed coloured. Standing on the fringe of the little wood, where the ground dipped and then cleared into rough pasture, Will could see the darker green of the many rings that marked the grass there.

In one of those rings a young woman was dancing – his mother, Moll Swayne. She carried a baby in her arms and sang as she danced. Her voice was high without being shrill, it was light and far away – it was a fairy voice, Will decided, just as the ring in which she danced was a fairy ring.

Will's sister, Delphi, sidled up to him and leant like a blown feather against his side.

"Wun't she scare away the Pharisees, Willow? She never danced the like before, did she now?"

"The babby makes her happy," Will said. "She sings to the little folk so they'll make the babby strong. So they'll never come stealing and put one o' their own in his place."

"Like they took Rowan," Delphi said, nodding sadly.

Will knew that Rowan, an earlier brother, had simply died, but he smiled and nodded and Delphi was content.

The sound of a cart approaching along the summer-baked track, the rumbling wheels and the tired clop of horse's hooves told the brother and sister that their father was returning from a day's hard work. Delphi ran to meet him. A second girl, small and skinny, scuttled out of the shadows and ran after her. Will stayed where he was, watching his mother and faintly smiling.

The moon grew paler and yet stronger. Now it was a beautiful boat without sails, drifting upward, growing smaller and at the same time more brilliant. Whatever had been touched with gold now blackened; the shadows streamed from the forest trees, losing their magical colour. Will had spent all his twelve years without a roof to his head and he had seen many moons shining on this countryside – but never one like this. The night seemed to fill with the love and longing his mother was pouring over the baby – like holy water from a font. Not that Will knew much about such things.

Behind him, Will heard Delphi's light high voice.

"Our mam's dancing in the moonshine."

Their father answered, quietly and gently:

"She dance where the Pharisees dance. Yon's a fairy ring she treads in."

"Shan't they mind?" Delphi insisted, somehow uneasy.

"Mind? Why'd that be? Why'd they mind their own queen a-dancing there?"

Will turned, then, and saw Delphi's white face in the moonlight, gazing up in amazement at their father, while the smaller girl hung about his waist.

2

"Is mam the Queen of the Pharisees, master?"

"So I've ever thought her," Sim Swayne answered. He glanced at Will. "Don't you say so, boy?"

"Pharisees", in these parts, meant fairies, the little people – though the blind preacher sitting under the oak outside the village had told Will that Pharisees were ancient, proud men, written about in a great book. Will knew better, and although he had never exactly considered that his mother might be the fairy queen, he knew there was something strange and magic about her. So he smiled at Sim and nodded.

"She'm Queen of the Pharisees," he agreed, liking to please his father.

"So she is, and I always said it, and all of you here is the Queen of the Pharisees' children." He was looking beyond Will and smiling. "And here she come," he said, his voice soft and loving, "bringing us your own brother."

Moll came swiftly to Will, bending towards him, holding out the baby.

"Take him, Willow. Take this babby brother and carry him for me. Hold him gentle and let me dance a measure wi' your father."

Will took the baby and held him. The moon shone on the little creature's wrinkled, anxious face. What cares had he brought with him from whatever world he came from, and would he forget them soon? Will put his hand on the puckered forehead as if he would smooth it. Had he looked like this in his first days in the world?

"He look like he got a bat's face!" Delpi said.

"He's a brother," Will answered, and he sounded solemn.

3

Two nights ago they had stopped in the little wood and made their firt and settled, as they did night by night in one place or another. From moonrise until almost moonset they had waited for the brother to be born. Then, when he was safely in the world and huddled up in the old shawl that was little more than rags, they all sat round in a close, awed circle and talked of what he should be called.

Will had been born alongside a river's edge and Moll had named him Willow. A churchyard was where Delphi had first seen the light, and on the nearest tombstone was the name *Philadelphia* – not that either Moll or Sim could read it for themselves. It was the sexton, coming to chase them away, who had cried out in fury – "And close alongside the last resting place of good Mistress Philadelphia!"

Will's second sister had been born at that change of dusk into night that is called fairy light, and Fairlight was her name. There had been others – Rowan, Rose, Holly – but they had all died. After Fairlight, who was now six years old, there had been no more babies, so that this new one seemed particularly amazing and important. The moon had been bright when he was born. Only one star had managed to shine.

"Star shall be his name!" Moll had said.

She ran now from her dancing and took the baby back into her arms.

"My pretty Star – my midnight Star – my only Star!" she cried; and bent over his poor ugly little face with a smile that told the rest she found him the most beautiful thing in the world. Sim put his arms round her and whispered something in her ear. She laughed,

4

setting her cheek against his. No wonder he called her the fairy queen, Will thought, watching them. Her skin was clear, her hair golden, her mouth full and red – but for all that, she had black flashing eyes that spoke less of a fairy mother than of some gipsy king, of some magical marriage between the two of which she was the daughter. She was plump, generous. Unlike Sim, whose handsome face was marred by gaps in his teeth, Moll had all her teeth save one. That one, when it suddenly began to ache, Sim had pulled out while she hopped and squealed and wept as the blood ran down her chin. Teeth are bound to be chancy things at the easiest of times and the life led by Sim Swayne, by Moll and their children could not be called easy.

There was no place they could call home. They had no roof and no chimney. They lived by wandering. The woods and the forest and sometimes even the wild seashore were home to them. Half tinker, half pedlar, Sim lived by mending pots and skillets, pans and pail handles and trivets. He sold nails purchased from the forges round about, and scythe blades sharp as swords, and knives and hammer heads. He sold, also, the wooden pegs and birch brooms that Moll and her children knew how to make. All these were carried in the cart that was pulled by old Brownie, and in the wet and the winter they either huddled under the cart, or, if their stay was to be longer than just one night, Sim would build a shelter of boughs and bracken and sacks. Once, in a fierce December, snow so piled upon their hovel, that they were caught like coneys in a warren – there was hardly a hole large enough to let them breathe, but it was all as warm as a palace.

As they moved now from the clearing and made for their night's rest by the fire, Will stumbled over something on the edge of the wood.

"Hey – look, master! Deer horn!"

Sim took the antler from him and turned it in his hands.

"That's the best of a half head – short of a tine or two. That'll have dropped from a fallow buck, surelye. Must've lain long – it's near enough polished ready for working." He turned it in his hands, lovingly and respectfully. "Well, none shall say he got'n poached by Sim Swayne!"

"What'll 'ee make on it?" Delphi asked. "Shall it be to handle a knife?"

"Two knives and still some. The rest make a fine handle for a hazel-wood staff. I'll carve a whistle in it."

"What for a whistle, master?"

"Why – to summon the Pharisees, that is your mam's own kin."

Moll laughed and the laugh changed to a yawn. She leant against the cart and suckled the baby, while Fairlight settled by her mother's knee and went to sleep. Now Delphi yawned and then Will. One by one they sank into sleep under the bright night while owls sped above them, busy with hunting. Last year's bracken, still lying in this untrampled place, heaped well into soft enough beds. There was no difficulty in sleeping soundly and dreamlessly on this familiar ground . . .

"Where'll we go now, master?" Will asked his father next morning.

At this time of year they rarely stayed more than two or three nights in one place. Because they had no roof of their own, no door to slam and bolt, it was easy to feel threatened. Sim always took care to cover his tracks; he might leave some secret store dug into a favourite resting place, but there was never so much as a half-burnt twig, a smear of wood ash, to show where they had rested. Sim knew, and Moll knew, that there was always some danger for wanderers such as they were. They might be seized and hauled before the justices and punished for having nothing; they might be sent out of some towns with blows and abuse, even whipped to the parish boundary. Sim plied a trade and the contents of the cart proved it, being full of hammers and nails and knives, sheets of beaten tin and lumps of solder to be heated in the small cauldron. There were also hanks of tow and twists of waxed thread, peeled withy for binding birch brooms, and many small carved boxes that housewives pounced on to hold pins or trinkets. It was the cart and all its treasures that stood between Sim and danger.

"Where'll we go, then?" Delphi cried, echoing Will. "Shall it be – that place?"

"That place" was in the deep forest, set upon rising ground so that the water drained away well. In some other time men had dwelt and worked there and left their mark upon it. Will liked it better than any other place he knew; Delphi, too – and even Fairlight, who was a shade witless; or scarcey-witted, as they said in those parts.

"Shall it be that place?" Will persisted, as Sim, busy about matters of his own, did not answer.

Without looking at his son, still preoccupied, Sim managed a reply. "Where else?"

Will grinned and Delphi squeezed his hand, while Fairlight did a little skipping dance. Only Moll sighed, rocking the baby, who seemed to cry a lot.

"There's a tedious long step, husband Sim."

"Slow'n easy," he answered her, his voice soothing. "Room for you and the babby in the old cart. Brownie'll pull you gentle enough, you'll see."

He smiled and Moll smiled back, but pouting, unusually languid. Last night she had danced in the moonlight but now she seemed weary. It was as though, after so long, she had lost the way of babies and was wondering, now that the first excitement was over, how best to keep Star well and content.

"I should'a bin born a lady, husband. Oh then how dainty I'd lie! All in a great silken bed and nurses to hush the babby."

"But you'm Queen o' the Pharisees, Mam!" cried Fairlight. "An't a queen a lady?"

"Who-so said that," replied Moll, "had best get me a crown o' gold. Real gold, mind – not fairy stuff that turn to dead leaves by morning."

The day was brilliant after the brilliant night. This was the best part of the year to be on the road. Laden brambles choked the hedgerows, the berries sweet and juicy. There were elders decked out with their sharp fruits, that looked like careful clusters of black beads. Along the edges of the forest tracks crab apples were plentiful, ripe enough to shower down when the wind blew. There were nuts and mushrooms, rabbits and squirrels – Moll knew how to stew a squirrel tender as chicken, and how to bake a hedgehog in clay so that when the hard case was opened the spines were peeled away. There was plenty of clear water, the springs bubbling and sweet, and sometimes Moll sent her children to beg milk at a cottage door. Mostly it was freely given, for they had learnt how to stand shyly and smile – and Delphi's smile was likely to charm even a resistant heart; she looked indeed a fairy's child.

From spring to summer, then, there was not much to complain of in such a life. But when winter came to howl through field and forest then truly all was bleak.

They were not thinking of winter now, as the sun grew higher and the day increasingly warm. Now Moll sat in the cart with the baby on her knee and he slept. All around them the pots and pans and nails and hammers kept up an incessant clatter and chatter as the old horse plodded on. Sim walked at Brownie's head and Will walked after the cart as if to protect it from all attack. Delphi walked with him, but sometimes ran forward to speak to her mother and smile at the baby. Fairlight darted about, now beside Sim, now plucking at Will's sleeve or grabbing Delphi's hand; or dawdling to snatch a handful of blackberries, then rushing after them, cramming the berries in her mouth as she went till half her face was stained purple.

"Stop by at the widow's," Moll called to Sim. "She'm a good soul for giving the young'uns a drink o' milk."

"I have it in mind," he called back.

Widow Tester lived in a cottage whose eaves stooped almost to the ground on one side. Her husband had built the place with walls several feet thick, and he had built good barns and byres and styes and been a flourishing farmer in his own small way. The fire that he lit when first he built the hearth had gone out only once in all the years, and that was when he died and his widow sat weeping. It was certainly burning now, for a wisping smoke plumed out against the blue summer sky and there was a smell of smouldering peat.

The widow heard the cart and was at the door before it had stopped.

"You got the new'un, then?" she called to Moll. "What's the name to be this time?"

"This is my son, Star," said Moll, looking down at the baby's ugly face with love and pride. His eyes flickered and he blew a bubble or two but slept on, twitching a bit.

"Such names!" Widow Tester cried. "They'll never get your childer into heaven! Take 'em to the parson, Goody, and see 'em baptised in a Christian manner."

"One day when parson come handy," promised Moll.

"One day – one day," muttered the widow, but without any malice. "Come to the byre, little heathens. Daisy just calved down and there's a draft o' poad milk for any as cares."

The first milk taken from the cow after calving was called poad-milk. It was a mystery how Widow Tester's cows calved at any season of the year, but it was accepted as the work of her sister who lived some miles away and was known as at least a wise woman, if not actually a witch.

In the byre itself, there being no dairy, the milk was standing in big bowls, three of them, and all with a fly or two drowned or drowning. This did not in any way discourage Will and his sisters. They seized the dipper and drank greedily.

"Leave a drop for the mam!" Sim cried.

When they had done, Widow Tester took them to see the calf and they all stood round and stared at the spindly little creature.

"A blackberry calf," the widow said, adding in excuse, "and none the worse, if I'm asked. Any more'n you might, Goody Moll, who've just given birth to a blackberry babe."

Moll looked quickly at the baby and then at Sim. She was frowning and pale. A blackberry child was one who might fare poorly, the first weeks of his life moving into the cruel winter.

"He'm fully strong," she said.

"Aye, for sure," the widow answered, "And so shall all they be proved wrong who say otherly ... Where're you bound?"

"Maybe finding where we'll over-winter," Sim said. "We know the best place. We'll be snug."

Widow Tester looked from one to the other and seemed uncertain whether to speak. At last she said:

"There's naun but old straw in the barn. You could do worse'n winter there."

Sim smiled and touched her hand.

"That's true and good neighbourliness, Widow. But I doubt we'd breathe proper indoors."

"Go your ways, then. The thatch won't fall for lack o'company. Remember where it stand, friend."

She was not a smiling woman but her voice held more than mere smiles. She stood watching as they moved off along the dusty track, shifting at last into the shadow as they came to the fringes of the forest. The track narrowed, the trees stepped closer, and now Moll and Sim and their children had vanished into a different world. It was a world which Widow Tester, though she saw it beyond her door every day, would not care or dare to enter.

2

THEY spent that night down by the ponds. Men were working down there, but they were used to families such as Sim's, who came at dusk, paused to sleep and eat and were gone again soon after sunrise. Besides, Sim Swayne was known to such men, iron-workers and blacksmiths from whom he obtained much of his stock. There was iron-smelting in progress on the far bank from where Sim chocked the cart wheels and unharnessed Brownie. There was a great roaring from the furnace and every so often flames shot high. They would be working all night, noisy and sweating, for they were halfway through a founday – that stretch of days during which the molten iron must run without check. Further along the pond bank there was charcoal burning and the fumes breathed hot and choking on the light breeze, so Sim made his camp with care.

On the wide water, three swans floated. It was almost dark by the time the fire was made and a rabbit skinned and into the pot. The small fire reflected the greater glare from the furnace and between the two the swans moved like ghosts. Then came the hissing and steam of cooling iron. Two heron which had been fishing late, rose at the sound and flapped away.

"Goodly here, too," Sim said, as the smell of the rabbit sneaked from the pot and the children clustered, eager for the time when it would be ready to eat.

The baby was quiet, and now Moll's anxiety longed for it to cry.

"Is he sad, Mam?" asked Delphi, peering at him.

"Aye – sad," her mother answered. She patted and rocked him and he wailed a little and dribbled milk bubbles down his chin.

"Ah, my poor Star!" cried Moll.

"Wun't he twinkle?" Fairlight asked.

Delphi screamed with laughter and the rest joined in, and after that they all felt better.

They moved on soon after dawn next day. The iron was still running, the men still sweating. The heron had not returned and now there was only one swan.

"Soon get set in," said Sim. "Soon get to that place."

"When, master? When?"

"T'morrer, boy."

☆

THE weather stayed fine and the ground was hard. It was not so many miles across the forest, but the going was obstructed and often dense. Where a whole standing of trees had been cut for burning, scrub had quickly sprung and now knitted and tangled with brambles and the tough bines of honeysuckle. These rougher spots might have been avoided if Sim had not preferred to move with as little fuss as possible, taking a longer way if that were the less obvious. They passed few dwellings, for these were mostly huddled on the forest fringes, the waste edge that was outside what had long been the king's hunting ground. There were always men about, however, moving secretly, almost silently, in that secret place. They might be fugitives in hiding, or perhaps disbanded soldiers now without occupation, or simply forest people about the

14

business of woodcutting, felling, clearing – and this might be quite lawful and sometimes not.

At one time, far away, they heard the thud of a water-driven hammer beating out iron; and coming by one forge Sim paused to bargain over a bag of nails. The walls of the forge were covered with goods – bits and bridles and horseshoes, lengths of iron chain, arrow heads for huntsmen and great keys to fit into huge locks; and bolts and hammers, and scythe blades finely honed. It seemed a place of enchantment to Will and Delphi.

Then they were on their way again, and no later than mid-afternoon, they reached that place.

"Still the same," Moll said, "Nothing change. Soon be settled in."

They stood together, Sim at Brownie's head, and gazed in a satisfied way at what seemed to be altogether theirs. It stood on rising ground, guarded by great yew trees. Once at the brow, the ground flattened into almost a circle. They had gone there first because there was so good a spring gushing into a rocky pool below. Another time as he cut through brushwood to gather fuel for the fire, Sim had come upon the remains of some sort of building. Men had been here, lived and worked. Only fragments of their quarters remained. Neither Sim nor Moll could know how ancient the remaining timbers were, and their true interest in the structure was that enough still stood to make a good shelter. They dragged over them the great cover that was always carried in the bottom of the cart. It was the most necessary of their possessions, made of sacking stitched together, the whole spread of material then being coated with pitch. The pitch had often to be renewed, for the cover cracked in its folds after a while – but when it was in good shape, it held off every drop of water that fell upon it. It was almost as important as the cart itself.

Sunlight beamed through the great trunks of the yew trees as Sim Swayne and his family toiled up the rough sloping way to the place of their choice. The children ran forward, trampling down the bracken, lush and tall, spreading now into fresh places which, last year, had still been clear. Soon it was flat enough to make a soft green mat and there they would all sleep in this fine dry weather. The trampled bracken had its own strange scent, not sweet, like hay, nor sharp like straw, but juicy, heady. Ahead of this bracken spread, the ground was flat and open enough to make a fire. Sim set about that before anything; Will skinned the second rabbit of the pair Sim had caught yesterday; Moll tossed it into the pot with a handful of dried herbs; Delphi and Fairlight began taking necessary things from the cart – knives, two wooden pails for water, a crock of chicken fat.

Suddenly Delphi shrieked out, "What's here? "What's here? See what I found!"

It was a loaf of fresh-baked bread, and with it a round pie made with apples. It was easy to recognise Widow Tester's secret generosity.

As the afternoon wore on, so with every minute they grew more comfortably at home. The pot began to steam, the fire crackled, Moll sang to Star, Fairlight gathered more and more fallen wood and made a pile of it in a handy place.

"Shall us go brambling?" Delphi asked Will.

"Aye – so's you don't eat all that's picked!"

"And fetch the water, Willow," Moll called after them.

Since last spring, Will had become water carrier and fetcher and it made him feel far from his childhood and of importance in his world. But he would not be done out of scampering with his sister as the sun began to decline and the blackberry bushes moved into shadow, so that the fruit would soon need to be groped for. It was a long way yet to the end of the year but this evening, as will strangely happen at harvest time, there came the merest hint of chill drifting under the denser trees.

"Go looking after misheroons termorrer," Delphi said. "I know the place they grow. D' you know it, Willow, since all this long time?"

He nodded. "They're mushrooms," he said, remembering the blind preacher. "Speak proper, do."

"See there!" said Delphi, catching his arm.

A line of five fallow deer crossed the clearing and moved silently into the shadows ahead of them. Sim Swayne had told Will that the deer belonged to the King – but someone else had then told Sim that a king had had his head chopped off – so what king was there now, and whose were the deer? "Not mine nor thine," Sim had said, "save by right of hunger. Better starve in the open than hang for poaching. That's wisdom."

Distantly, brother and sister heard their mother calling.

"She need the water, Willow."

"Soon," he said, enjoying freedom, the coming dusk, the chance to chase and hide. He dashed away and found himself among the yew trees. The downward fall of the ground had caused them to bend outwards, and that side of the great trunks that took the air and sunlight had sprouted green almost to the roots. The close growth was like moss, like velvet – only Will had never seen any velvet, save the furry growth that covered a deer's antlers for a part of the year.

Will ran his hand over the yew trees' trunks, moving from one to another as if caressing them. He was so taken up in the delights of the place that he forgot Delphi and found himself alone.

All sound had died. He could not see the light of their fire nor hear any voice he knew. There was no hint of Delphi moving swift through the undergrowth, laughing because he could not find her, no call from any bird or beast. Will stood in a place he knew, that he thought of when he was away from it; but without warning, with a terrible sense of alarm, he knew himself to be a stranger. He was watched in wary silence by badger and hedgepig and birds just roosting – and maybe by those who had come here long ago, the men whose dwellings Sim had found and turned to his own advantage. And by what else? The preacher under the oak tree would speak of the eye of God, but Will had no understanding of that. His anxiety was more familiar. He knew beyond doubting that somewhere within this spur of forest some other stranger lurked – but with intent for good or ill he could not know ...

A bird broke cover above his head and flew like an arrow twanged from a bow, but with a harsher note. The shock of it made Will freeze in terror, then hurl himself wildly among the brakes, the bracken that gave cover for some way. Then he was plunging through whippy birch seedlings that snapped and snatched at his face and hair. Then at last he was close to the fire, with Moll sitting drowsing and Sim busy about dragging the cover over the useful timbers that Moll and Star might have shelter.

Delphi was already home and laughed when she saw him.

"I did tease 'ee, Will. I did beat 'ee home!"

Sim looked sharply at Will, who seemed unable to speak. Moll roused up, looked in his face and reached for his hand.

"What come to Willow?" she asked, soft and coaxing.

"Naun," he answered, and pulled away his hand.

"Fetch us water, then. I told 'ee that long ago. Hurry, now, for there's barely light."

Will shrank, and heard his father say, "Leave him stay. Bring me the pails, Delphi maid."

Sim hung the pails on the wooden yoke that was slung beneath the cart when they travelled. As he passed Will he paused unexpectedly and kicked over a piece of ground that was soft and loamy, its surface broken. A scatter of small bones, rabbit or chicken, showed white on the dark forest floor.

"Maybe others come this way," he said.

He spoke softly, almost to himself. Without a glance at Will or any of them, he went off with the pails. It was almost night time now and the shadows received him. Will wanted to run after him, but held back – the feeling of dread that had swept over him as he stood by the great yew trees still menaced him. It stayed with him, even after his father had returned, even after the meal was eaten, crusts of Widow Tester's good bread mopping the cooking pot clean. And when he lay down to sleep, Will moved as close as he could to Delphi and Fairlight. So that all lay no more than an arm's reach from their mother.

During the night, Will woke often. His mother and the girls slept soundly and so did Star. But beside the fire Sim sat as if on guard against some danger that had never threatened them before. He whistled softly to himself as he sat there. By the light of the fire he was cleaning the piece of antler found on the edge of that clearing where Moll had danced in the fairy ring.

By morning, all seemed as usual. The risen sun shone sparkling in the dew collected by every spider's web.

"Go gather bavins for the fire,' Moll ordered Will and Delphi. "And watch you not fall in the water come you jump the stream. You get a drenching and I'll see you sorry for it."

Moll had a hard and stinging hand and it was often in use. Her temper flared into bursts of fury that sent her children scuttling, though they did not need to stay away for long.

The heavy dew stung their bare feet like frost. Will and Delphi skipped and shouted as they ran over long soaking grass and plunged into the thicket beyond the stream. There was never any shortage of firewood to be gathered there and they had their arms full within minutes.

"We'll not need more'n we got," Will said. "Let be, Delphi – we got heaps and plenty. Delphi!"

She was crouching over a big fallen bough of oak

20

and tugging at a smaller branch alongside.

"Delphi!"

"I saw summat – summat lying ..."

"What summat?"

Delphi plunged her hand through a scattering of leaves and scrabbled in the soft earth.

"Shiny ..." she said.

Will moved towards her and as he reached her side she sprang up, clutching something in her hand. She stood there in the bright sunshine, robins shouting above her head, and stared at her clenched fist.

"Show," Will ordered.

"Nay – I dursen't."

"Where's the sense in that? You found summat – then show summat!"

He gave her a shove and she tripped and nearly fell.

"You gurt booby!" she yelled. "I'll drop it! Leave me be or I'll chuck it in the stream – then you'll never know! It's my foundle – mine! I won't show it none but Mam or master!"

She kicked out at him. Her toes were hard as a little pig's trotters against his shin. He yelped and hopped – and set his foot on a holly leaf and yelped more than ever.

Delphi seized her chance and rushed away, screeching out in excitement – "Mam! Mam! I found summat shiny and Will wants steal it from me!"

The noise made Will glance anxiously over his shoulder. They were all taught to move quietly in quiet places, to speak soft lest any be near to listen. Delphi's high excitement scattered the morning and sent birds into flight and squirrels chattering. What if someone heard – was listening – came near and spoke

21

in a boding voice ...? Will did not know who might do this, or why, he only knew that, mysteriously, the place we changed – that it might well be shared ...

"Undo thy fist, then," Sim was saying. He had caught Delphi by the arm and was prepared to give her a good shake. "Show – show – open, you mawkin. Open that first!"

Very slowly, as if she held a butterfly that would be gone as soon as seen, Delphi unlocked her fingers.

On her dirty palm lay a coin. It was not dull and earthy, like other coins they had found here from time to time. It glittered richly.

"Gold ..." Sim said, almost whispering, "Come here, Moll, my lady. Has your majesty ever seen the like?"

A gleam came into Moll's eyes. She whisked the coin away from Delphi and bit it as hard as teeth could bite.

"Gold," she said, as awed as Sim. She looked at it wonderingly. "I'd say here's a guinea, husband. A whole gold guinea."

It was a fortune. Will and the two girls clustered round and the treasure was passed from hand to hand. When it reached Delphi she held it hard, crying out that it was hers – hers.

"That's for all-us," Moll said firmly. "Give it here, you wicked thief."

Delphi dashed off, and began dodging among the trees with her mother chasing after and Fairlight squealing behind them.

"Shall it buy a new horse, come poor old Brownie go?" Will asked.

"Nay. Nor even a satin gown for the Queen of the

Pharisees, Willow. As well let Delphi make a hole in it and hang it round her neck. We never can spend such." He saw the boy's puzzled disappointment and smiled a little. "Think, Will. Who'd ever believe Sim Swayne come honest by a golden guinea? There'd be telling and blaming and up before the justices – and prison at the least and hanging at the worst. We dursen't ever think to spend it, boy."

Moll came marching back with Delphi howling beside her and Fairlight grizzling in sympathy.

"Think now," said Moll, her arm thrust through Sim's, "think what it shall do for us! Come next sheep-fair it'll be a ribbon for me and hoods for my girls. And you and Willow shall have a fine neckercher apiece, Master Sim Swayne. We'll spend half and keep half and have a treasure by us for another day. We'll buy marchpane and barleysugar sticks and a little coat for my Star. Oh – that shall be a fine day – a fine day!"

Her cheeks were flushed and her black eyes sparkled. She had hardly ever in her life seen so much money.

"Leave your dancing and singing, wife. We never dare spend a farthing of it – and that you know well."

Moll swung away, clasping her arms about her as if her disappointment was a terrible pain within her. She knew that Sim spoke true and would not budge from his wisdom, but the misery of it made her then clutch her face with both hands and pull the hair over her eyes.

"I think most," Sim said quietly, "on how it come to lie where Delphi found it. It's bright and clean – else she'd never saw it lying. It never lay there long. It come from some pocket yesterday, day afore that. Not much longer. That mean others come lately to this place. Then – who? Where they lie hid now?"

Will felt again that creeping chill at the back of his neck. None held the key to this place. It was anybody's place. It had seemed theirs, theirs only and on other living soul's. Now that pretty bit of gold had changed everything.

Sim took the coin from Moll. He wrapped it in a piece of old skin and bound it round with twine. Then he moved up to the summit of the mound where, only last year, he had found under a vast wooden floor a whole well-fashioned chamber. It was as dry as old bones; it smelt of silence, Moll had said. There they had made a great store of nuts and dried mushrooms, of deer meat smoked for keeping, of hard cake that Moll made by pounding honeycomb with a measure or two of flour – whisked away from a distant mill. All these things Sim had smeared round with clay and given the package a quick sealing at the fire. Then they had closed up the store's entry and left it for another time. They had many such stores, but all of a more modest sort.

Now to all this Sim added the golden guinea, digging on the threshhold, which was of beaten earth, and making a secret scratch or two to remind him where it lay. The rest stood round as he did this, Delphi snivelling to see her treasure hidden away, and the baby crying with persistent, unconsolable fury – as if he, too, knew rage and disappointment. There was something sad and terrible about the moment – as if it promised worse to come.

There was little merriment that morning. The

24

golden coin had somehow destroyed their peace. Even Fairlight was silent. She held the baby for Moll, rocking him in an absent-minded way that Star seemed to like, for now he slept quietly.

"Best get set to brooming, this noontide," Sim said. "There's handles for stripping, Will. I'll be off for withy."

They had left, beside their food store, a great mound of birch cuttings for broom making, together with twenty or so cut lengths of hazel for handles. Will fetched these and Moll and Delphi hauled the birch branches. They set to work almost silently, dividing the birch into suitable bundles for each handle as it was stripped. These bundles had then to be bound with long strips of willow – the withy that Sim had gone to seek. None knew better than Sim Swayne how to bind the twigs evenly around the handle and to tie them so tight that they never came adrift.

The day was very still. Here and there the trees were changing colour and down in the bottom was a sudden swathe of bracken that had turned yellow overnight. From where they sat at work, Moll and her children could see the forest spreading on all sides. A few paces away, old Brownie cropped lazily, swishing his tail against the flies. The cart was standing no more than ten yards from the fire where the smell of gentle stewing rose enticingly. The sun shone. Sim returned with his willow wands and joined in the work. It was a familiar, peaceful scene. Yet whoever had dropped that gold coin seemed to tread among them, and they suspected him. Perhaps a rogue who had stolen and then lost and would fight to reclaim

... Or else some gallant, with a pocketful of gold coins, who could surely spare it – but might be some great lord, or lord's son who would drive them furiously from this place where he had rights and they had none ...

"Two more and we've score," Moll said. "Shall you be glad of a dish o'stew, Willow?"

"When'll it be deer meat?" Will asked. "Shan't we go take a hunk o'deer meat out the store, Mam?"

"Ask your father. He's to decide."

"Tomorrer," Sim said. "Maybe."

The baby woke and cried for feeding and Moll took him from Fairlight. As she did so, the sun went in and at once there was the chill of autumn about them. And more than autumn – for once the warm was over they were bound to think of winter, waiting its turn to tease and harry them. The cold and wet, the struggle to find food for all of them, the bitterness of threadbare clothes and chilblained fingers and toes and sometimes ears and noses – all these shifted near as the sun went down that day.

They sat in silence over the stew when the time came, gnawing the bones of pigeon and squirrel until there was not even the smell of meat left.

Then Moll said, knowing Sim's thoughts though he had not spoken them, "There's the place by the river – after the pool wi' them otters. Good shelter there. The cave – remember?"

"Ground's too low, my lady. Too low and wet for winter staying."

"The old house, then?" she said.

She looked at him anxiously. The strange nervous anticipation that had touched all but Fairlight and

Star, seemed then to move among them like a real presence, touching them lightly on the brow, on the nape of the neck. Moll did not take her eyes off Sim's face as she waited for his reply. He stayed silent, reluctant to answer.

"Better be so, husband," Moll said – and she spoke gently, knowing of his disappointment, childish as Willow's – for he loved this place and was pround of his careful hoard that could see them all through the winter.

"Aye," he answered her at last, heaving the words up with difficulty. "Better be so. Surelye. Best set about it. Let it be the old house. Take all we may carry from the store and go our way. Best so."

Now it was spoken. That there was some danger. That others had moved, maybe still moved about this place. That they could be near at hand – somewhere in the dense forest, even sheltering among the yew trees ... Watching, waiting for some chance – and to do what?

Sim roused himself. "Will – you and Delphi get down to the hazels and pull as many nuts you can. Watch the babby, Fair. Your mam must needs help me carry."

"I can carry, master," Will said. He could hardly bear to see his father's disappointed face, but he knew, as clear as light, that they must go. Perhaps those men from long ago, who had dwelt and built here, leaving so much behind – perhaps their spirits had come again?

"Do's I bid!" his father snapped.

Delphi tugged at Will's hand, pulling him away. She was as white as a daisy. She, too, knew that they must go, and without too much delay. Before dark came again, they must go.

"What is it?" he asked her, impatiently, as if to send fear flying by speaking of it.

"Come quick – quick!" was all she would say.

They got two bags of hazel nuts and another of crab apples, though most of those were bruised.

Then, as they turned back towards their resting place, it happened.

They heard Fairlight scream.

3

WILL turned instantly and began to run. He heard Delphi's wail of fright and protest behind him.

"Wait – oh wait! Don't leave me!"

He glanced back over his shoulder and saw her standing like a little stone figure, her hands clasping her white cheeks, her shoulders hunched.

"Will! Will! Come 'ee back! Never leave me!"

She ran a little way, then, stretching out her hand. He grabbed it and pulled her after him. Ahead of them, Fairlight's cry had merged into shouts and screams, less of fear than of fury – Moll's voice above the rest – she was all but bellowing, and there was little left in her voice of the fairy queen.

Delphi fell and Will was obliged to pause and help her up. Tears were now streaming down her face.

"What happen? What happen? Shalln't we hide, brother?"

"Pick your silly feet up and leave bawling! Come fast after me. I'll needs get ahead."

"Will . . .!"

He pulled his hand from hers and began leaping up the bank towards the place where they had made their shelter. As he reached the summit he saw what seemed at first a score of strangers – movement everywhere – struggles and shouting – terrible danger . . . Then his vision cleared a little and he saw that besides Sim and Moll there were just three unknown men. One, dark, heavy, with a great black beard, had leapt on Sim's back and was shoving him to the ground. Another was tugging at the cart, pulling it away fast.

The third, shouting to the others to make haste, had Brownie by the halter and was clearly waiting to get him into the shafts. Brownie, alarmed by the noise and the smell of strangers, tugged and bucked like a two-year-old.

Moll was hanging desperately on to one side of the cart, so Will threw himself at his father's attacker, pummelling and tearing at him. As Sim went down, first on one knee and then flat to the earth itself, Will sprang on the man's shoulders and hit him about the head so that he roared, and then seized him by the sides of his beard.

The man abandoned Sim, who lay prostrate, and with a great heave, shoved Will away. But now Delphi had reached them, and she ran in and kicked at the man's shins and scratched and clawed at the backs of his hands and any bit of flesh she could reach, pinching and twisting the skin at his wrists like some terrible mad little animal.

Somewhere in the background, Fairlight was clutching the baby and screaming spasmodically.

Moll suddenly left the cart and rushed towards Delphi as the man seized her and seemed about to hurl her away into the bracken like a stone or a bone or a clod of earth. Moll sprang in her turn and now it was her nails that went into action, searing down the man's face so that the blood ran sharp and red into his beard, and then grabbing towards his eyes as if she would have them out, so wild was her rage.

The instant Moll left the cart, the second man had hauled it fast down the slope and already they had practically harnessed up Brownie. Will, aching now, partly with despair, went back to the attack. This time he seized the man about the ankles and almost brought him down.

But this enemy was like old tough leather bound and stuffed into the image of a man, and Will was far too light to do him much damage. He found himself kicked away, rolling towards the gorse bushes a little below. He would never save himself from those villainous spines, and he put his arms over his head. He landed with his face against the earth and his shoulders taking the worst of the thorny branches.

He lay still, his head spinning, and tried not to sob. Behind and above him he heard a terrible clatter and shatter as Brownie, sent on his way with a wallop, tilted the cart and upset half the contents over the rough forest floor . . .

Then suddenly everything was quiet, even Fairlight. His mother was stooping over Will, then pulling him from the gorse and fondling and rocking him; he was crying after all.

"Ah my lovely boy, my lovely boy," she murmured to him, over and over. "You done valiant, my fine Willow."

Now her voice was the one he loved best to hear, the voice of the Queen of the Pharisees, and he clung to her as he had not done since he was four or five years old.

"Come now," Moll said then, "come to your father. He do sorely need comfort."

Sim was sitting with his head in his hands. He seemed to be unhurt, but his pride hung about him in ribbons. Delphi was crouching beside him, peering into his face but afraid to touch him.

"Fetch water, Delphi," Moll ordered.

Delphi shrank. "I dursen't."

"Go with her, Will – take each a pail. Quick now."

Will took Delphi's hand and they ran to the spring, the empty pails swinging.

"They'm gone away now, Delphi – never fear 'em."

"Did they come find the golden piece?"

"They got a deal more'n it'd buy."

Delphi began to weep quietly. "Poor Brownie – poor Brownie – shall they treat'm right?"

"Treat'm like a horse," Will said, gruff and hating. "Only our master treat a horse like he was a friend."

The spring water ran clear into the pails, but into Delphi's there fell a salt seasoning, for she could not stop crying. They turned for home, Will carrying both pails and slopping more than he cared to see, for he was still shaken and unsteady.

"Look there!" he shouted out suddenly "See what happen? The cart must have tipped more'n ever it done till now. Look what fell out!"

A good half of the cart's precious contents lay scattered on the rough ground, all muddied with trampled undergrowth.

"Run on, Delphi! Run on and tell what we see!"

Her tears ceased, she dashed off. Will set down the pails and ran to the scatter of possessions tipped from the cart. The yoke was lying there and Will pounced on it and set it on his shoulders. It was much too big for a lad of his size, but he slung the pails and staggered on his way. Ahead of him he heard his father's shout and knew that Delphi had given her news.

Roused from his misery, Sim came running, with Moll not far behind. They flung themselves down and began gathering the treasures.

"Here lies my best ladle!" Moll cried, seizing it and brandishing it.

"And the pot with the bent lid, Mam," Delphi said, eagerly joining in. "And Fair's doll that master carved – that was mine till I give it."

"There's nails and needles here, Sim. Look here, husband – what's nails for but to hammer up a new cart? What's needles for but for stitching and mending – not that I see any yarn. Come, Sim Swayne, and see how we'll soon get goods again for selling – and solder for mending – and all things needed."

Sim was sitting on his heels. He looked pale as ashes but he smiled at Moll.

"Brave as a lion, my lady," he said. "Sweet as a fairy and grand as their queen. I were born a seventh son and fortune touched me, surelye, first time I met wi' her ... Come now, my children and their mam, gather up all here and see how best we'll manage."

Soon Moll had made the fire burn brighter. She had fed the baby and put him to sleep under a bramble bush. The pot was hanging and the stew was steaming. As she looked after these matters, Sim made two packs of all they had found, rolling one in the sacking cover they used for shelter, and lashing the other around with the rope which had fallen from the cart with all the rest. These, which he balanced cunningly, he slung on the yoke for easier carrying. As soon as they had eaten, they stamped out the fire and scattered the ashes so finely that none would know any man or woman or child had dallied there.

When all this was done, they turned to go. Sim had shouldered the yoke, Moll had picked up the baby. Will and Delphi each carried a pail packed full of food from their store in the underground chamber. At the last, Sim decided that they should take the golden coin Delphi had found. It was dug up from its hiding place and released from its covering, so that Moll might slip it into her bodice, where there was a slit that she had fastened with a pin – it made a little pocket between the stuff of the bodice and its lining.

Delphi stood looking around her.

"Shalln't we ever come this again?"

"Never," Sim answered. "It was a place chosen and now it is cursed. See you don't look back as you go."

"Never?" Will asked his mother, not quite believing.

"One day – one day. When the good drive out the bad and so it shall."

Sim strode on. He was still pale and Moll walked close by him, as if to help him. She had the baby tied to her in the old tattered shawl. That left her one hand free and she carried the stewpot packed with knives and oddments - they were wrapped in a green bodice that was her best – it had been thrown on a bonfire burning on some village green, and she had snatched it – it was a little singed about the neck.

Behind Moll came Delphi and Fairlight, each with a burden beside a packed pail, and after them all, in his self-appointed position of guard, came Will. He could not believe they would not see that place again.

They came now into a part of the forest they hardly knew. The going was hard until suddenly they came on a little river, neither wide nor deep, but pleasantly curling and sweeping among reeds and grasses. Every so often along its banks there was a small clearing, with grass cropped by coneys and bushes nearby bowed down with blackberries. In such a place they had spent some time one summer when Will was little and Delphi only just born. And here they decided to rest again. There would be plenty of rabbits, also heron were likely to come fishing and a heron was a good meaty bird in spite of having such long legs.

They stayed in this place for three days and nights, seeing the moon dwindle while the weather held fair. At night, the mist rose swirling from the river's face so that they awoke with almost dripping-wet hair. The baby coughed.

"Here?" Moll asked. "Do we stay here?"

Sim sighed. He still seemed tired. It was the cart — the terrible, dangerous loss of the cart that made him brood and scowl.

"No place for staying," he said. "In winter the river could rise and swamp all. Frost hang here late and early. We mun go elsewhere."

"The old house, then?"

He still frowned, he still hankered after the cart. Without it he could be called a vagabond. It was as bad for him to lose his cart as for a king to lose his kingdom.

"The old house ....?" Moll repeated.

He nodded without speaking.

Next day they headed south-east. Here there were more tracks and they made good progress in spite of the weight of stuff they lugged with them. On the evening of the second day, they came to the old house.

☆

WILL and Delphi had been here often before. They ran to it, dumping their loads on the track, rushing about the rooms and passageways as if to discover what might have changed in their absence. In fact, they could hardly be called rooms at all, nor the house a house. It was like a picture of a house, its full proportions drawn on the ground. No walls remained. The place had clearly been destroyed by fire, but how long ago would have been hard to discover; even if Sim and the rest had ever thought of asking or cared about the answer. The scorched stones had obviously been quarried by those needing building materials, and carted away, so that at last nothing remained but vaults and cellars, carrying on their heads a memory of a dwelling. Some of these underground chambers were filling bit by bit. Earth was washed into them by winter rains, carrying seeds of birch and ash and even oak. Very soon only those who knew the house existed would be able to find any trace of it. Then those people would die and the seedlings become trees to smother the final memory. Then none would know.

On their last stay, Sim had covered the well before leaving, shoving a great stone across the mouth.

"Best see if the well still run," Will said to Delphi.

They made their way through brambles and even nettles, that will always grow where a dwelling has stood. The stone still covered the well's mouth, but honeysuckle had crept from a nearby clump and spread tentacles to conceal the well. There were bright berries on the honeysuckle now, and still a few flower sprays. The stone was enormous and Will looked at it uneasily. Would Sim be strong enough now to drag it away so that they might draw the water?

"Here come master," Delphi said. She ran to Sim

and took him by the hand.

"Open the well, master," she ordered him.

Sim plucked back the honeysuckle and shoved at the cleared stone.

"Stand beside and give a heave when I shout," he told Will. "It grown back into its ground, Will. Not every man know how stone take root like any tree." He smiled at Will. He had not spoken of the struggle with the strangers, and how Will had fought and beat about the man attacking his father. But now he said, as if to excuse the smile, "You come a useful size and strength these last days, Willow Swayne."

Pleasure turned Will's ears red. He grinned in his turn. What pleased him best was to hear his name called in that way. He knew he had no honest right to it. He had never been baptised and his parents had never seen any great necessity to be decently joined in proper wedlock. Willow Swayne – it sounded fine – almost a name for a gentleman's son.

Sim was now peering into the well. "It run clear as any other time. Let the pails down, soon's you may."

Since a good part of their belongings were rolled in the tarred sacking, they had to be unpacked before any shelter could be made. Sim cleared the bracken and birch from the cellar they had used before, and the sacking was stretched and rigged. Cut bracken was spread like thatch on the cover, and then the shelter almost disappeared into its surroundings.

For the second time, Sim turned to his son.

"You make as good a fire as any, Will. Get to it, then. I'll go after meat."

It was very peaceful in the old house. The sun declined, birds sang; Delphi went wooding and came back singing, too. Fairlight sat close by Moll and watched the baby feeding. Over the last days, Star had seemed quieter and more content. This evening he cried, not angrily, but in wailing protest.

Sim returned with four pigeons and flung them to Delphi and Fairlight to be plucked. He frowned over the crying baby.

"He'm doing poorly again. What come to him, Moll?"

Moll looked up from her study of the baby's face and she looked ready to wail herself.

"Not enough milk come to him, husband. Where'll we get other?"

Delphi dipped a finger in a crock of honey that had been among the food in the store. She put the finger in Star's mouth and he was silent and sucked contentedly.

"He do tickle like ants!" Delphi cried.

The fire was burning well, the pigeons were plucked. Sim stuck them on twigs and roasted them. They were small and cooked quickly. Then everyone sat round gnawing at the bones and spitting what they could not chew back into the fire. The fire hissed and sizzled into a blue flame. It was not much of a meal, even though Fairlight ate little. At the end of it, Will and Delphi were still hungry. But they were glad to be here – it was a good place, even if not as good as that other. Dusk changed to dark and Sim stirred the fire to make a better light, for he had set about working at the antler. Sometimes he looked across at Moll. His eyes were anxious, but when she looked in turn at him he always smiled as if to reassure her. The last thing Will saw before he dropped asleep was that look between them. He loved his mother and would always work and care for her so long as she needed him; but he would die for his father.

☆

S$_{IM}$'s hand on his arm woke Will hours later. The last of the now misshapen moon shone in his eyes but he knew Sim's finger was on his lips.

"What's it to be, master?" Will asked in a whisper.

Sim shook his head but pulled Will to his feet and then moved away, beckoning him to follow. Soon they were out of hearing of any of the others who might wake.

"Bring the pails, Will, and follow after where I lead."

"Where we go?"

"To fetch milk for the baby – where else?"

Sim used the word *fetch*, but it could only mean *steal*. Will was used enough to taking what could be got no other way. The midnight, the crooked moon defiantly bright cutting through it like a sword, gave suspense and deep excitement to the moment. Will snatched up the pails and followed where his father led. They must be on the way to that farmstead on the distant side of the nearest village – and that was some miles from here. It was a source they had enjoyed often. The cows grazed on sloping ground and at night they gathered in a fine hollow under a clump of aspen trees.

Deer moved swiftly but without any sound, as Sim and Will made their way through scrub and young birch. The moon had slipped a good way towards the horizon by the time they came to a few scattered dwellings. The place was too small to have a church, it was more a forest settlement than a village, with a smithy and a pond. Last on the track that wound through it was the farm.

A high moving mist had now draped the remnants of the moon and the light was flat and colourless. The air was so still that a vixen calling ten miles away was heard clearly.

"Wait till I whistle," Sim said to Will. "Keep close. Gi' me the pails."

He moved away and the strange night swallowed him.

Will stood where Sim had pushed him, among a clump of young birch trees alongside the main track. Standing there among them, Will felt that he too grew into the ground, becoming as he did so a part of the swelling forest. He strained his ears till they sang. Somewhere away down the hollow field ahead of him he could swear he heard the sound of milk swishing into the pail. At the same time, he heard a badger's worried grunt and he spoke to it without thinking.

"Go quiet, Brock," he said.

It seemed to Will that he stood there an age and still Sim did not whistle. Then the silence shattered into bits as a dog broke into wild barking. Will heard it run to the end of its chain, and the clanking and rattling told of its weight, and of the size of the dog on the end of it.

Sim appeared from nowhere, milk slopping as he ran.

"I lost the half! Here – take one pail – there's still a good measure. Quick about it!"

They divided the milk between them, Sim taking

twice as much as Will. The dog was still roaring and now there was a man shouting.

"Off wi' us, boy! Follow close as maybe!"

He had disappeared almost before Will could take in what he was being told. He followed as fast as he could and as quietly. He was afraid of falling, of upsetting all the precious milk. He was so busy watching his feet that he struck his head against a low branch. He felt it bleeding.

Soon the sounds behind them were lost and once more they were sharing the place with its true dwellers. So then they could make their way more slowly, glad of a chance to breathe easier.

"You got a good milking, master," Will said.

"I made a great botch on it. Next time we needs find another herd. That hound'll be loose about the place, many nights to come."

"Where'll we find other beasts handy?"

"We'll find 'em. We must find 'em. Otherly that babby'll get to starving – and then he's bound to die." Sim looked sideways at Will. "You'll come along o' your father, eh Willow?"

"Aye, master," Will said, shifting the pail to his other hand and wondering how far it would have to be carried next time.

4

THE next day, since it was obvious he would have to travel further to find milk, Sim set out soon after noon.

"Best this time you stay and guard the women," he told Will. "Them that took the cart and poor old Brownie have others like 'em. There's villainy all about in these times."

"I'll care for Mam and my sisters," Will assured him, feeling taller every minute. "And also my brother, Star."

"Aye – the little brother," his father replied.

He smiled slightly. Then the smile faded and he sighed. He turned and went off into the quiet forest. For a time Will could see where he travelled. The high fronds of invading bracken that found good growing here where a whole house had died, were stirred and fidgeted by his passing. Then he emerged from the stretch of bracken and was seen briefly shifting in among scrub birch and bramble.

At last all was still. Will called Delphi and they went off to pick mushrooms. There must have been many beasts when the house still stood, with its farm and byres. The ground stayed rich and the white buttons of the mushrooms dotted a whole stretch of grass cropped short by rabbits, where once there would have been cattle or horses. Now all that was forgotten.

Moll had a little crock of chicken fat carefully preserved from various stolen birds. She put some in a pan when Will and Delphi returned, and set some of the mushrooms to sizzle. A good handful she put aside, saying they should be for Sim.

"This night we'll roast a bit o' the smoked deer meat, and misheroons with it. And termorrer morning, Willow, early, fetch me a mortacious great lot o' water. I needs must wash the clothes."

Delicious as were the fried mushrooms, Will and Delphi groaned. Wash day meant lying low in a naked condition until the clothes had dried. None of them had much more than one lot of clothes to wear, summer or winter, day or night. Such use made them hard to clean – and they were so old, anyway, that each washing left fresh rents for the wind to blow through.

"Not termorrer!" Will protested. "What if master be away and an enemy come and the only man nigh you lies in hiding?"

"We sent our enemy packing," Moll said firmly. "This place come quiet and still and no voices heard. But if they come – you dash out, naked and yelling, and they'll take you for a hobgoblin."

"Wash Delphi's things first ..."

"They'm all to be done – don't ever doubt it. Weather's going over. Brambles is dropping to the flies and the trees and the brakes are changing, We'll go clean into winter, will ye, nil ye."

"Star's crying again," Will said, to divert her.

Then he was sorry he had mentioned so obvious a matter, for his mother's face changed. She seemed to grow old and haggard as he looked at her – more like a witch than any fairy queen.

"Must we lost 'un, Willow? Must we?"

Fairlight began to whimper dismally and tears

rolled fast down Delphi's cheeks. She and Will had seen other babies die, and they, like Star, had looked waxy and wizened.

Suddenly there was Sim coming up the bank to them and smiling widely. He carried the one pail only half full – but at such a timely moment none would complain of that. Moll's face cleared instantly and she ran towards him with her arms outstretched.

"Where? Where? How little time you bin! Did you milk the forest trees?"

"I come on a hovel I never see before – though it stand so close here. There was three goats tethered."

"You took from 'em in daylight? That were bold. Did none catch you about it?"

"The goat I milked let out a bleat. An old woman come to the door."

"An' see you there?"

"She call out loud and cross, Moll. But I see how it went for her. Blind – or near to."

"Ah poor soul," said Moll, but without very much conviction. She could only be more concerned for her baby than for an old blind woman whose face she did not know.

Sim had come home so fast that the milk was still warm. Moll took the baby on her lap and dipped a rag in the milk and held it for Star to suck. He turned his face away, screwing up his eyes and making a fearful grimace. They were all crowded round, anxiously watching; he had never tasted goat's milk before.

"He hate it," Delphi said dismally. "There's naun worse'n goat's milk. That's what he think. Don't he, Will?"

"Be silent," snapped Moll.

Then she held Star to her own breast and dribbled the goat's milk towards him and at last he sucked. After a bit he settled and fed, his hands that were almost transparent clenching and then spreading, his toes curling and uncurling. After a while he fell asleep. His eyelids flickered and he smiled in a tipsy way. Moll sat on and on, rocking him gently, unwilling to set him down lest the wailing begin again. The afternoon wore away, and then Star was handed to Delphi and the rocking and the loving continued until it was Fairlight's turn. And so, turn and turn about, they held him all through dusk and on into the night. And all that time he slept sound as a mouse in its hole.

Sim went again to the blind woman's hovel and this time he took Will. The tiny dwelling, little more than a room with a roof and a chimney, huddled in a small clearing. Perhaps once the clearing had been bigger. Perhaps the old woman's husband had stolen it from the forest years ago, building the house hurriedly, getting a fire burning and smoke rising by dawn – so that he had a squatter's right to remain. But it was clear by the way the scrub and the brambles were creeping back that the unknown man must have died some time ago.

Sim approached the dwelling. The door stood open and he peered inside. The old woman was sitting on a three-legged stool close up to the miserable fire. She called out at once, "Who's there?"

"Goody," said Sim in his softest voice, "I'm here to beg milk for my babby. He do well on goat's milk."

"Little good in begging from a beggar," she said

roughly.

"Then let me milk a measure and my son here shall cut wood for your fire. Thatways we strike a good bargain."

She rose and groped towards them as they stood on the threshold.

"I see naun much of faces now. But your voice tell you're no evil man, so be it. Is the babby sick?"

"The milk shall cure him," Sim said, positively.

So each day after that the milk was collected. Will set about chopping wood and hacking back the thick brambles where the goats before now had got themselves entangled. Though Star did not grow fat and energetic, he cried less, and would sometimes kick quite cheerfully and wave his arms. Sometimes Delphi took him down the little track that was now being worn to the blind woman's door, through the bright increasing autumn. Then the old woman, whose name was Goody Nye, took him on her knee and talked to him as though he were a grandson.

"Shall I mend the fire?" Delphi would ask. "Shall I get water and wash they crocks? There's cobwebs above the chimney – I'll give 'em a sweep."

And once Will found her sitting on the floor by the old woman's knee, singing some nameless song.

"There's a fine song I do delight in – that I sang come I were a lass. *Netting'n Knotting* – or some such folly. Sing it, maid – sing it."

But Delphi knew no songs with words, only strange tunes that she had learnt from Moll, and some she had made up for herself.

"Come termorrer and see you learnt it proper b'then," the old woman said, almost threatening. She

46

had caught a bad cold with a terrible cough, so severe that sometimes she leant against the wall, holding her side and gasping. "Why'nt my four fine sons come home to say farewell?" she muttered as Delphi left that evening to run home through the dusky forest.

Now the autumn lay well and truly over the forest, blazing into red, into copper, into gold. There was more in the way of fungus to pick than just mushrooms – though the most beautiful was the most venomous. Light frost nipped at each night time and in the morning the grass was almost white. And now the spiders' webs held more than drops of moisture where the dew had settled, for the frost hung in them like chipped diamonds. The nights grew chilly, and in the shelter Sim had made them at the old house, the Queen of the Pharisees' children huddled together for warmth. Without the horse and cart, how was Sim to get to any market to barter his goods for warmer clothes? With all the rest, they had lost, when the cart was taken, two ancient cloaks, tattered but still warm, and three old wool coverlets.

Sim grew troubled and morose as the weather became colder. The nearest town was several miles away and he must travel now with a pack on his back. He must either leave Moll and the children behind to fend for themselves, or they must all go tramping, their pace suited to the slowest. By now they had a good supply of besom brooms, of clothes pegs and woven baskets – but how to carry them all was a dreadful problem. Life without the cart was even more difficult than Sim had expected, and he was moved to positive despair – he had best cut all their throats, he said, and be done with the turmoil. Then he would look at Moll and see that this terrible threat only made her smile.

"Why do you smirk, stupid woman?" he cried.

"You've frit the little 'uns, Sim Swayne. Tell 'em quick what I know these many year – that you do nabble words that's as full of air as puffballs."

By now Delphi and Goody Nye were such friends that Delphi was allowed to milk the goats in return for a song, even if its words were not the right ones. Most days, Will went with Delphi and did some jobs about the place, for the little pasture was now cut back and clear again. They took the old woman a broom for her own, which pleased her. But most of all she liked to talk and to hear them talking.

"Is that brother Will o' yourn a fine set-up lad, Delphi?"

"He'm big and brave," said loyal Delphi.

"And is that sister a pretty maid," she asked Will, "wi' curls and blue eyes?"

"Come you speak of it," replied Will, in the grudging way of brothers, "she seem middling lightsome. Aye – her grows curls."

For the first time since they had known her, the old woman laughed, throwing back her head and clapping her hands together, so that brother and sister could not help but join in.

"God bless all!" cried Goody Nye, wiping her blind eyes. "All but as good as seeing to have a fine laugh!"

They laughed so much that suddenly the old woman clutched her side and cried out.

The laughter ended. "Are you hurt, Goody?" Delphi cried in alarm.

"Nay — nay, maid. Well enough for the way things are. Get home — but come again termorrer."

☆

THEY sat round the fire at dusk and there was a stew with mushrooms and a duck that Sim had taken from the big pond that filled the bottom a mile or so away. In the pot, too, Moll had flung a handful of herbs picked that morning. They were peppermint, dandelion and garlic, and to these, the last of the year, was added a handful of juniper berries. The stew was hot and tangy and made Fairlight sneeze.

"Old Goody Nye laughed so merry she took a stitch to her side," Delphi told Moll.

Moll glanced across at Delphi through the firelight which both lit her face and shadowed it. She looked solemn.

"What happen then?"

"I said were she well — and she say, Well enough."

Moll shook her head. "She see an end though she see naun beside."

"Shall she die, Mam?"

"Aye — soon ..."

Moll always knew about such things, so after that Will and Delphi and sometimes Fairlight, went more often to visit the blind woman. Delphi went to watch over her, though this might not be said aloud. She had become a friend and they could not remember any other, save Widow Tester. At night, before he slept, Will found himself thinking of the blind woman, and closing his eyes he wondered how the world must seem to her. Then he remembered, too, the blind preacher sitting under the oak tree, and the strange things he had said – things that were a mystery to Will, that sounded sometimes fierce and threatening, sometimes cheerful and promising.

At Martinmas the weather changed again and was fair and warm – St Martin's summer, Goody Nye called it.

"Who's he to make it so?" asked Delphi.

"He were a great and holy man that lived at the start of time."

"And he make it sunshiny, then?" Delphi insisted, but sounding now a little mocking.

"Not him, he don't. The good Lord God make the weather and one year, t'other year he make it fine at St Martin's time."

Delphi looked at Will for help, but like her he had not understood a word of what the old woman was saying ...

That day, as if she had tested them and not been disappointed, the blind woman opened a great chest that stood almost the length of the far wall.

"See what's here," she said. "My husband, long years gone, carried this from a great house burned down. I kep' what it holds for my sons' wives, but they never come this way."

The chest was full of clothes – of cloaks and mens' leather jerkins, of ladies' gowns, hats with feathers, sashes and shawls and collars of lace. The lace was yellowed, and over all the cloth and the velvet and the leather was a patching of mould and mildew, so long had they lain in that damp place, against the wall between whose cracks the rain crept in, standing on the beaten earth floor where the goats, let in from the cold, made wet puddles to add to the rest.

"Never saw the like, did 'ee?" Goody Nye chuckled, knowing instinctively how Delphi stretched out to touch, how her fingers curled covetously.

"It's magic treasure," Delphi said. "I'n't it, Will?"

She looked at him slyly and sideways, as her hand closed on a feathered cap. She took it out and put it on her head, but this the blind woman did not know.

In sudden fury, Will snatched the cap from his sister's head and shoved her away. He returned the cap to its resting place and shut down the lid.

"One day, Goody," he said to her, "your sons shall have brung their wives after all."

"Better be soon," she muttered.

Hurrying back home to their own ground, Delphi broke into tears of rage and hit out and kicked at Will as she ran beside him. Will sullenly remembered such a fault of his own – when he had stretched out to take a snoule of bread from the blind preacher – but he had known and caught Will's wrist. "Remember the wrath of God!" he had said, low and fierce. Will had not troubled himself to find out what this meant – there was no one he could ask and be sure of the right answer. But the words had remained with him and now he turned and spat them at Delphi.

"Remember the wrath of God!"

It sounded terrifying and Delphi's tears turned to sobs of fright. She fled away from him, vanishing so completely that he was alarmed and yelled after her.

"Where you go, Delphi Swayne? Come back, y'silly mawkin!"

He would arrive home without her and his mother would rage, for he was supposed to care for his sister as carefully as a shepherd lad with a pretty lamb. But she was ahead of him and already bawling out her tale to Moll.

"Did you say such a thing, Willow? To your own sister? Where'd you hear such dreadful words? Wrath o' God, indeed! Take care how you mouth of those matters."

"It was the preacher at Staglye," Will said sullenly. He was also bewildered by his mother's shocked expression. Better if he'd spoken of the Devil, for him they had most certainly been told of.

"Listen till I tell you," Moll said severely. "'Tis certain only that God put us in this world and he'll take us hence. That's writ down. But what come in between it's best for us to settle and not go talking about him. And so's you keep a kind heart the Pharisees'll see you safe enough."

Will could not have questioned this, for all he heard was confusion. He found it hard indeed to imagine how the blind preacher under his oak tree could be anything at all to do with fairy matters – indeed, he had already made it very clear that his Pharisees were quite different from Moll's.

"Why'd that preacher say about wrath, then, Mam?"

"Get on stop your yammering," his mother said sharply. "Rain's coming. There's the smell on it a'ready."

☆

THE rain came at midnight and fell fiercely. The ground was hard and beaten where the house had stood, in spite of the scrub that had grown to cover it. This was a great benefit in dry weather but when the rain came down it was another story. There was nowhere for the collecting water to run except into the cavities below, where Moll and Sim and their children sheltered. Damp crept into every corner, the rain put the fire out, the clothes that Moll had washed so carefully had never seemed so threadbare and useless.

In spite of this, only Will lay awake. In the first part of the day, when a faint light lifted the sky high above the treetops, the rain ceased. Then all was silent save for the dripping of water, the slither of dead leaves now brought down by the rain's battering.

Will lifted his head and looked cautiously round him. Still they slept, Delphi with Fairlight huddled behind her and clasping her round the waist, Star in Moll's arms. Sim was next to Moll, his head against her shoulder, his right hand lightly curling round the haft of a knife . . .

Will moved away silently. He left them all sleeping and sped off through the frest to the blind woman's cottage.

5

WILL knew perfectly well that he was going through the near-dark to steal from Goody Nye. It was the worst possible day to have been offered both the opportunity and the need. He thought how he had rebuked Delphi, and he thought about the mysterious wrath of God. But the fact was that Will had often enough crept up to dark dwellings, mostly as Sim's shadow, and taken what was available – a chicken, a handful of eggs. Moll, too, never missed any sensible opportunity – she could even take honeycomb, for part of her magic was the power over bees.

In the strange stillness of the rain's ceasing the cry of owls, often so gentle and friendly, now sounded both eerie and cruel; the cry of hunters whose prey might be no less than a scared and hurrying boy. He almost felt their talons grasping him, lifting him as eagles might and carrying him away. Will wished he had not come. If he turned now and raced for home he might get back before they missed him. But then, ahead and a little below him, he saw the cottage.

She need never know, he thought, if she was sleeping. She would not mind, he assured himself. If she woke, then he would either run for it or tell her he had come early for milk. He saw that only a thin wisp of smoke was rising above the roof. The fire must need mending. Then he would fetch wood and make all bright and the old woman would be grateful. Perhaps she might want to repay him ...? "The big box," he would say, "the warm cloaks ... the boots, Goody ..." And he would not need to steal, after all.

"Take what you may," she would tell him.

Now he was at the door and his hand on the latch. He tried to open gently but the door resisted. What if there should be a bolt? Then the door gave way a little. There was something propped against it, some stool or other heavy object that the widow had shoved there before she slept. Will put his ear against the narrow opening he had won, expecting to hear snoring. What he heard was the light whickering, blowing noise of the three goats sharing the widow's lodging. He had forgotten they would be in.

Again Will shoved at the door, persistent but careful, afraid it might suddenly fly open, disturbed already by the presence of the goats, expecting any second that they would break into loud bleating. Now the door opened a handsbreadth – just enough for him to peer inside. He crouched on his haunches and tried to discover what it was that prevented the door's opening. As he accustomed himself to the dark inside and began to see a little, a tiny flame on the hearth suddenly flared, magically lighting the place.

He saw the flame reflecting in the goats' eyes – and he saw that Goody Nye herself lay across the threshold, barring his way.

Now very much afraid, Will slid his hand through the crack and touched her. His fingers found her face and he plucked them back fast. Her face was cold and stiff and still. Will knew she was dead but he could not quite believe it. He had seen dead animals; he had seen the little dead brothers that Delphi could not remember. He had seen a bunch of bones hanging on a crossroads gibbet and been told they were the remains of a felon, but he had never seen any ordinary grown person lying so cold and quiet.

His eyes filled with tears and he trembled. Almost as still as Goody Nye herself, he crouched there clutching his hands together as if to warm them. Above and around him the day began. On the little worn track to the cottage door a badger grunted homeward. The three goats, their heads close together, gazed pitifully at Will as if they knew what had happened and that their lives were now changed.

The goats had to be released. Will gave the door one more mighty shove; there was just room for them to escape. They had to jump over the old woman lying there and he shut his eyes until it was done with and the goats out in the open and bleating loudly.

"Give over that hurley-balloo!" Will roared.

His voice, roughed as it was by tears and a strange anger, startled the goats so much that they ran all together and stood blinking their long pale lashes – then the boldest lifted its lip and bleated back at Will, but softly as if it feared what might happen next. Will turned away, knowing he must find his father quickly. In his haste, Will forgot to drive the goats inside the shabby hedge. As he ran home, sobbing a little under his breath, he knew someone followed and hardly dared turn his head. But only the goats came after him, anxious to be milked and unwilling to let him go.

As Will came towards the old house, he saw everyone up and busying themselves – Sim at the fire, Moll lazily yawning and scratching, Delphi returning with an armful of kindling, Fairlight dancing the baby.

Moll saw him first.

"Where bin, Willow? Didn'ee get water?"

Delphi gave a scream of laughter.

"Them's Goody Nye's goats come follerin'!"

Sim glanced up at Will and saw more there than the rest could see. He rose from coaxing the fire and held out both hands. Will rushed to him and fell against him, crying in a voice of the utmost misery:

"She'm dead. Old Goody. Poor old Goody Nye — she lie dead at her doorstep ..."

"Hush, then," Sim said quietly, holding him. "Is that truth?"

"Aye, master — truth it be."

Moll stared at Sim. "I knew so — and she did, too. Not long, she said — or summat like. She rest easy, surelye."

☆

THEY milked the goats before they went to see about Goody Nye. Then they led the animals back and tethered them lest, Sim said, there might be eyes to see and minds to wonder what they were doing in another place. In the depth of the forest were always those who could move without being watched — it was they who did the watching and knew how to profit from it. Word could travel here though it might never be spoken.

Sim and Moll between them shoved the door open and went inside, stepping over the poor woman's body. Will and Delphi, Fairlight and Star remained outside. There was a watery sun. The day was not cold.

Delphi slid her hand into Will's and squeezed it hard.

"Now us'n shall have 'em, Willow."

He did not see fit to mention the wrath of God, too painfully aware that he had had his own plans.

"Have what?" he asked.

"Them she showed ..."

He did not answer. He felt ashamed of Delphi and therefore ashamed of himself. He was puzzled, uncertain of how he should behave. He felt a sorrow that seemed at once foolish and necessary.

Presently Moll came from the cottage. She looked thoughtful though quite easy in manner. She said that Sim would dig a grave for Goody Nye in her bit of pasture and so she should lie forever peaceful within the forest.

"It can't be soon done. Willow – take Delphi and seek what foundles you may to deck the grave – there's still a sprig or two to lay wi' her. Set about it, then."

Fairlight wanted to go with them, but Moll needed her to hold Star. She was always puzzled when Will and Delphi went off together and left her, but too vague in her mind to bother about it for long.

They took a battered old trug to carry whatever they might find – and it would not be so very easy to find anything as late in the year as this. Everything was battered and dulled by last night's rain, which had saturated all that stood or crept or twined. But gradually as they moved on their way the forest gave up a score of secrets. There was a twig of wild cherry still holding its bright leaves, and this Delphi plucked and laid first in the trug. There was gorse blooming, as gorse will always bloom, and they each managed to detach a painful sprig or two. There were berries on the holly but they knew better than to pick that –

holly belonged to the Lord of the Manor, the Earl himself; it was said the deer needed it for winter fodder. True or false, they would take no chances. By the stream, in the bank's shelter, was a spread of dandelion, great lusty gold blooms opening as the sun strengthened, leaves dark and strong and good for eating. Delphi chewed at one as she moved on towards the spinney ahead. The water ran between rotting beech roots and here they had great good fortune. Honeysuckle had climbed over trees long dead and there were not only berries but a number of blossom heads still sweetly scented. Here, too, they found a single woodrose, its petals as frail as dead butterfly wings. On the far bank, almost at the mouth of a foxhole, Will grabbed at a clump of heartsease, though that indeed was very battered. Besides these, growing keen as the search continued, they chose hart's tongue fern, some fronds of red-gold bracken, the tangled thready heads of old-man's beard, three stalks of willowherb, the seed heads unbroken and rosy. As they turned back, for they were wandering further and further away, Will gave a shout of pleasure. On the crab apple tree they had almost passed he suddenly saw a bunch of mistletoe. To conclude all, as they crossed the clearing ahead of the cottage, Delphi picked up a fine heron's feather.

In the bottom of the old trug then, there seemed to lie all the forest in little.

"That's well done," Moll said. "Take Star for a spell, Delphi. Let Fair be rested. Will, best you go help the master."

Sim had chosen a corner of the pasture for the grave. The rain had softened the ground but he had only an old battered shovel and his two hands to dig with. He was looking grim and tired.

"Like as not there'll be stone to hit," he muttered.

Will went into the cottage. He found an old cooking pot and working beside his father he shifted the earth as it was dug.

"You done well," Sim said, echoing Moll's words. It was dark, it was midnight and they were working by lantern light before the hole was big enough. Then old Goody Nye, her long span over, could be laid to rest and covered with the earth she had trod for so many years.

Now Delphi laid on the earth, just about where they all thought the old woman's heart might be, the gorse, the honeysuckle, the woodrose, the heron's feather and all the rest.

"Shan't it be dark for her?" Delphi murmured, snivelling a little.

"Not near so dark as when she'd no eyes to see with," Sim said postively; but he did not explain what this might mean and it seemed to Will that, anyway, her eyes were tight shut now.

"Ah, poor soul," said Moll. "God and the Pharisees keep her safe – like I told you but yesterday, my Willow."

They went indoors after this, and though it was deep night, Sim made the fire bright and Moll found some bits of food the old woman had stored; a piece of venison smoked in the chimney, cheese made of goat's milk, a loaf. When they had eaten, they shut the door and slept by the fire.

☆

THERE were plans to make.

"Shall us live here?" Fairlight asked, when it was day once more.

"Ask your father," said Moll. She flickered a glance at Sim. It was easy to see that he was restless, that he was bound to make a decision and did not know what it had better be. "Shall us live here, husband?"

"Maybe yes, maybe no," was all he said.

"If we go," said Delphi, "shall us take the clothes?"

"Clothes? What clothes, maid?"

Will said sharply, "A box on 'em. Along the wall. Where Star's been laid." He was angry. He did not know why he had not spoken of the lovely hoard, since it had filled his mind since he first set eyes on it. He had been ready to steal from it and so had Delphi, and that was nothing new in their lives. But because he had been thwarted by the sad old woman lying across the door, he now felt reluctant to handle the stuff.

But Moll had leapt up and moved Star quickly into Fairlight's arms and opened the heavy wooden chest. She let out a wild cry and plunged both hands inside and dragged out huge heaps of garments.

"Wool!" she shrieked. "Feel 'un! Wool – and tight woven. Where from? Where from? They never could've been poor Goody's own."

"She say her husband, long ago, took 'un from the house that was tumbled."

Moll said, sharp and eager, "That were our house – the old house. They could as well bin ourn."

Will muttered, "She kept 'em for her sons' wives. Ask Delphi. Her four sons, she said." He sounded sullen and confused. Why should it be harder to steal

61

from a dead friend than a living?

Moll was singing with pleasure, one of her own wordless songs that were so easy for her children to understand. She held up gowns so grand and so covered with mould that no one, ever, would wear them again. She brushed eagerly at the patches of damp, then shook out the garments one by one – and one by one they fell into rags and then into little more than dust.

Then she came to big warm cloaks and began to dole them out among her family. But these, too, had been ravaged, this time by moth, and two or three fell to pieces.

"But the rest is ourn!" she cried. For in spite of the damp and the moth, the mould and the mildew, enough was left to keep them all warmer than they had ever been in any winter they had known. "Ter-morrer, come the sun shine proper, these'll hang airing on every bush!"

"See none's by, then," Sim muttered. "There's more about of that kind took the cart. It needs wars to keep such busy beyond the seas."

Moll gave a shrill laugh, maddened by his stolid manner.

"And so some'd say of thee, my pround Sim Swayne – wi' naun of his'n to prove he's bettern' any other vagabond!"

"Be silent," Sim growled.

He went outside. They heard him pacing about out there.

Moll sighed and kicked at the fire. Then she snatched up a handful of stained lace from the box and put it over her hair.

"Am I a lady?" she demanded.

"You'm Queen of the Pharisees," Will and Delphi said as one.

But she sighed again. "Roof and walls never did seem right for him. Nor often for me — save for warmth and the way the babby frets."

She looked at Will as she spoke, and then quickly away, but not before he had seen the sadness in her face. Once again, he thought of those other brothers.

That night, Will could not sleep easily, but constantly woke and stared about him. It was stuffy indoors in spite of all the cracks in the walls, the draught under the door. With five of them and a baby there was no longer room for the goats and they had been banished to the cove, the lean-to byre alongside the back wall; there they bleated dismally. Each time he opened his eyes, Will saw his father awake in the firelight, working on the antler and the hazelwood staff he had selected for it. Then the light touched the cracks in the window shutter, the cracks in the door. Sim was gone, Moll already stirring, Delphi gone milking. In their new place this day began as every other day had done since the beginning of time.

☆

SOME time short of noon, when they were all beginning to hope for food, whatever it might be, Moll suddenly lifted her head and stood very still, listening.

"D'you hear it, Willow?"

He shook his head. Sim, who was chopping firewood by the hearth, rose and went to the open door and listened in his turn.

"Naun to hear," he said.

"Aye, husband – the horn!"

She in her turn went to the door, pushing it wider. Far away as the hunting horn was calling, the deer knew. Five passed at speed, heads up, eyes starting. A ripple seemed to pass over the forest, as vibrant as the notes of the horn itself, that sounded so merry while it heralded flight, terror and blood. This was the very first time since they returned to the forest that Sim and his family had heard the horn and waited for the hunt to rush by, a bounding tide of men and horses and hounds – but the forest had not forgotten, nor ever would.

With astonishing speed the hunt grew nearer, the horn now blasting and strident. But though the huntsmen moved fast, the horses were keen, the hounds snuffling, they had not yet scented any prey worthy of their care. They rode out into the clearing ahead of the cottage and paused there to determine their course, the horses snorting and impatient of the check, the riders calling to one another, shouting and surmising.

The hunt was led by a handsome man of middle years, a shade portly, wearing a feather in his hat and high soft boots to the thigh. His gloves, too, were fine and fringed at the cuff; his doublet, also of leather, was supple and easy. Many hunts before this one would have supplied all that soft skin.

"It is the Earl, surelye," Sim muttered. "The Lord o' this Manor. Come inside."

They had all run out to see the sight, and now the wailing protest of Fairlight, the questions of Delphi and Will's reluctance, all wove into a movement and a sound that attracted the attention of the fine gentleman. He turned to look in their direction, then spoke to the servant at his elbow. The man answered and then his master pulled round his tall black horse and rode towards the cottage, the servant following.

"Stay, then," said Sim. "Too late."

The gentleman reined in a few paces from the cottage and called to Sim in a strong commanding voice.

"Is this not Widow Nye's holding? Where is the old woman?"

Sim reluctantly pulled off his cap.

"She come to die," he said.

"Address his lordship decently," the servant cried.

"She did die, my lord. And fully old, too. Eighty year."

His lordship seemed unexpectedly moved by this news – it was said, indeed, that some landlords knew and cared for their tenants.

"And blind so long, and patient. Well – God give her a good rest ... Are you her son?"

"A friend. Come lately here."

His lordship seemed to consider. Would he demand, what right have you here? His face, though strong, appeared not unduly stern. His glance shifted to Moll and lingered.

"The old soul paid her due in good rich cheese as I recall," he said. "See the goats come to me without delay."

He gave a brief nod and turned back to his huntsmen. The horn sounded then and hounds which had been ranging the nearby woodland gave tongue. Some heavy beast, a fine stag no doubt, crashed through the undergrowth and was away. The Earl and his servants made ready to spur off with the rest – but then his lordship checked and spoke to the servant riding with him. He rode on himself while the man turned back to Sim.

"Come with the goats by noon tomorrow, fellow. His lordship is minded to have you as tenant for the old woman's holding. Come to the manor, then, and ask for the steward. And see you do not leave at home what you owe in dues."

Now indeed he left for good. The clamour continued near at hand and then was drawn away into the distance. Utter stillness remained behind. None dared breathe, then at last the forest stirred again. A fox ran close by the stream; three deer picked a nervous path down the far bank then vanished as shadows vanish when the sun goes in. After a further pause, birds flew uneasily among the higher branches. A robin exploded into song.

"The goats?" Moll said, frowning. "Must'n have the goats? Whyfor, husband?"

"Who dies, his heirs shall pay the lord his due. That's ancient."

"We're no heirs of her'n, Sim."

"He thinks to do a kindness, my lady. To give us sad poor folk a roof to our heads." Sim laughed. "The gentry cannot live wi'out a roof to their fine heads!"

"But if he take the goats – how'll Star be fed? We needs must keep the goats. Shall you tell'un?"

"Aye – maybe."

"Maybe?"

"Leave me in peace a time – let me think."

Sim lived by instinct rather than by thought, so now he had a great effort to make. He moved away from the rest and stood with his back against a tree. He picked up a piece of fallen branch about a foot long, and brought a knife from his pocket. He stood slicing at the wood. By the time all was sliced away he would be bound to make up his mind; he would know what was best to be done.

Moll turned and went indoors, and after a little the others followed. Far away could be heard once more the horn's summons, the baying of the hounds — but the horn was a thread of sound, the hounds no more than buzzing insects.

"What'll come to us?" Delphi asked, moving close to her mother.

"He'll tell soon enough. Come sit by the fire."

They did as they were told and Moll in her soft strange voice began to tell a tale to distract them. It was about a king and his three sons, as most such tales are likely to be. The youngest son wed a fairy and the others, envious, plotted to kill him ... The story was never finished, for Sim came in.

"Best go from here," he said.

"Where to?" Moll asked, making no ado.

"Widow Tester promised the barn. There. We'll go to her and Star shall have milk enough."

"It mean a roof and walls, husband. Shall you bear it?"

"What I must, I may," he answered.

Then he was silent, as if listening to his own pronouncement. He put his hand on Will's neck in what was a hard grip but which the boy knew to be a loving embrace.

"There, Will Willow," Sim said. "Them's the best wise words I ever found. Let you keep 'em."

6

It took a good deal of the morning to make bundles
of their belongings. They used the cloaks and the big
kerchiefs for the bundles, in this way making one job
of two. Sim would carry two of these, the largest and
the heaviest. He had finished his antler-headed hazel
staff and would be able to grasp it to help him along
the way, which was rough and tangled. It was a long
way to Widow Tester and her barn and they had
much more than themselves to carry there. If Moll
regretted leaving the cottage she did not say so – only
Will even questioned Sim's decision.

"Shall you not see the lord's steward, master?"

"He'm no lord to me."

And then he drove out the goats to run as they
pleased. He shouldered his huge and heavy bundle,
grasped his new staff, his thumb fitting comfortably
round the antler, and without even calling any one of
them to follow, strode off.

Moll then gave her children each a burden to carry,
settling a load for herself that still gave a free hand to
carry Star slung in a shawl over her shoulders.

"Come now," she said. "I'll sing us a travelling
song."

She looked back once at the cottage and then followed after Sim, singing as she had promised, Fairlight at her side, Delphi and Will behind. And behind
them hurried the goats, unmilked and anxious to be
with those who had cared for them and would surely
do so again.

After an hour on the way, Sim called a halt. He

milked the goats and everyone drank as much as they could, rich and new as it was. They rested briefly and then set on their way.

"Shall the goats be led?" Will asked.

"Leave 'em decide. They're his'n or our'n. Let 'em choose."

Unburdened, the goats ran merrily, attracted by voices that they knew, now and again darting off to nibble at tufts of grass, to stretch their long necks to grab some prize from the scrubby woodland.

It was a fine day, warm in shelter but blustery in the open. As time went on the wind increased and going was much slowed, since the wind buffeted and plucked at the bundles they all carried. Moll had no more breath for singing, but the wind blew of its own accord through the whistle Sim had carved in the antler, and the stick whistled gently without his help. This pleased him and made him smile for there seemed to be magic in it.

Because of the wind and all that they carried, they had travelled wretchedly slowly, and by the end of the first day were obliged to stop at a place they knew from another time. Alongside a hollow whose high banks gave warm shelter, three separate springs dropped over rock and fed a clear deep pool. No one spoke much. They were all tired. It was tiresome to undo the bundles and take out what they needed for a night's stay.

Will had never before felt as he felt then, looking around him and knowing this must be left behind. The thought of the barn plagued him. He stared at this ground, the ground he knew as he knew no other, and all its creatures seemed to swarm there, blaming him for going away.

Not only deer and fox and badger, rabbit and squirrel, but all those smaller creatures he knew and noticed day by day without giving them much attention. Like shrews and harvest mice, bank voles and snakes and lizards, the bats, and the birds whose names he did not always know. And snails and beetles, spiders and butterflies and moths; and glow worms and crickets ... They ate baked hedgehog for that night's supper, as they had done on their last visit to this spot. But this time Will found it hard not to spit out the meat in disgust at himself.

Their second day's travel was easier. The wind had dropped a good deal and there was sunshine. Then in the afternoon all grew still. It became much colder. At sunset a hint of green in the sky promised frost. That was when they came to the forest pale and left it for those fringes where timber was scarce but much heather grew, that was good for thatching. A little ahead of them they saw the scatter of buildings where Widow Tester lived and where her empty barn waited.

"Do you rest here, husband Sim," Moll said then. "I'll go forward wi' the little 'uns." She smiled. "Best so."

He nodded, saying nothing – but he gave her a look that troubled Will, for he seemed to be wishing her good fortune. And what if that fortune were not good – if Widow Tester had changed her mind – if she had died, even, like Goody Nye, and a stranger dwelt in her place ... ? Was this what his mother had in mind? He longed to ask her, but dared not.

Moll settled Star more comfortably, took Fairlight

by the hand, and called to Delphi and Will to follow. They went steadily and rather slowly to Widow Tester's door, which stood open, displaying the little stair that led up to a chamber above – an arrangement so grand that it quite awed Will and his sisters.

As Moll stood at the threshold, Widow Tester came round from the back of the cottage, a pail in one hand and a milking stool in the other.

"God save us – Moll Swayne here again! Whatever come to you, my dear soul, that you look so frit and pale?"

"The babby," Moll said in a low voice.

"Not dead?"

"Nay," said Moll sharply, "for here he lie in my arms. But sickening – sickening. He need shelter from the sad winter that come so fast."

Though Moll spoke solemnly, there was a singing in her voice. There was also, faint and thin, just the hint of a whine, the whine of one who knows too well the rules of begging.

At this an anxious look came upon Widow Tester's face, that was much lined but healthy with hard living.

"Is it the barn, Moll? I do recall I said it stood empty."

At this point, as if taught the best moment, Delphi began to cry – and Will, as if learning from her what was best to be done, put his arms about her. As for Fairlight, thumb in mouth she clutched Moll's skirts and seemed to hide.

"Ah, dearie, dearie dear!" the widow cried. "Is Sim Swayne not here to speak for you?"

"He's hard by, wi' the goats."

"Goats? What goats?"

"There's three fine nannies follered us along the forest way. And will not leave us – eh, Will?"

Will shook his head, though he might just as well have nodded.

"They should'a bin tethered. Animals'll surely stray come they're untethered. Go call your father, boy. We'll need speak together."

Will went gloomily back to Sim, for by now all he wanted was to set down the bundle and rest.

"She change her mind," he said. "She say you come talk wi' her, master."

Sim shouldered his own bundle and picked up two more.

"Bring the rest and see the goats follow."

Will called to the goats and when he reached the stone wall that enclosed the widow's land, he sent them through the broken gate and lugged the rest of the bundles to the cottage door.

Inside by the fire, Moll was listening while Sim and Widow Tester talked.

"Things changed," the woman was saying, "and who's to know when such may happen? Stay as I promised – but maybe not all winter. My holding has been spoken for and seeing I am a widow I must get me a husband or else go from here. So I have chose John Penfold, whose wife die just lately."

"What of his holding, then?" Sim asked.

"His own son must have it, since now his time come to get wed. That place lie near the parsonage, so parson think best that Penfold and me should wed, too. It seem a fairish deal, for he's an ugly face!" She laughed. "But where'd I go, come I leave here, seeing

I've no grown childer to take me in?"

"What harm to John Penfold, with us in the barn?"

"None, Sim — none that I see. But men can be hard-minded animals. He'll be master here. It must be for him to say." Then seeing how they all looked, far beyond any pretending, she soothed them as best she could. "Stay — stay for now. It's not till three Sundays this Sunday that we'll get to be man and wife." Then she looked away and said, speaking rather fast, "If he say otherly and you take your ways — then I'll have care of the goats."

☆

It was an uneasy bargain and grew more so when, next day, John Penfold came visiting his intended. He was a square man, not tall, with curling hair that had once been red. He had a big hard voice. He stood in the barn and surveyed the scene with a look of stunned incomprehension. He did not speak. Whatever he thought or felt he was bound to swallow for the time being. Widow Tester was the tenant and had tenant's rights until she married her new husband.

The widow herself now displayed an anxious, nervy state of mind, as if she greatly feared the consequences of her impulse.

"I'll see his mind changed!" she cried. But she no longer looked them in the eye.

In their hearts Sim and the rest knew that John Penfold's mind, being narrow, would find it hard to turn. They did not care to admit this and did not speak of it. Although Sim might delight in being rid of roof and walls, for Moll's sake he would bear them, knowing her anxiety over Star.

There was a mass of old straw in the barn that made fine bedding. They made their fire in the yard and Sim hunted their food as always. They gave the widow goat's milk for cheese and she gave them loaves on baking day. If only there had been no John Penfold, they could have been snug and spent good working days on brooms and pegs to sell at the first market after the winter, when the roads dried and allowed more movement. But they heard constantly the arguing and anger between the widow and her suitor; and each time he called, on arrival and departure John Penfold came to the barn and, standing on the threshold, stared at them in silence.

Meanwhile the weather broke into true winter. If they were to go, they should by now have gone, Sim said gloomily. The days were exceedingly evil, wet and cold, the skies interminably grey except for blacker clouds that rolled and rolled, gathering ever more to spill upon the earth. With one of the moth-eaten gowns Moll made hose for her children, while Sim, mending his own old boots yet again, then made boots of a kind for Will and Delphi and Fairlight, using leather he had cut from the tops of high boots in the chest at Goody Nye's, boots too worn and indeed too big to have a use in their own right. Moll had snatched a pair for herself from the chest, and they pinched dreadfully, but now Sim used his skills and eased them for her.

"Now we got shod, do we move off?" she asked him.

He would only say, "When the weather lift."

The rain persisted. The fleas that bred in the straw seemed driven on by the damp to bite as no flea had ever bitten before. Fairlight was the worst bitten and the worst for scratching, so that she made great raw patches that would not heal on arms and face. Flies and midges might bite and sting when the family travelled through woodland and slept under the open sky, but they were clean and friendly compared with these indoor-breeding torments.

Though the winter had only lately struck at them, it being but the mid-part of November, already they yearned for spring. They all suffered something from the roof and walls, but Sim truly suffered. Moll and the children counted shelter worth some other discomforts and could endure even the fleas for the sake of keeping dry. But Sim would sometimes fling himself out into the yard and stand with his head back until it dripped with rain, his mouth open as if he would drink the sky dry.

Four days before John Penfold would claim his bride and move into her dwelling, the weather changed. A fierce wind blew from the north-west, the ground hardened so fast it might have been burned dry. Then in turn the wind fell away and all was silent. The clear sky at evening was full of frost and later the stars sparked and glittered. The forest felt the change. Will, out wooding on the fringes, knew that it hunched itself to meet snow.

"Now soon we go," Sim said. "We'll not wait to be bidden. He'll have us out and there's naun to be spared by doddling."

Moll looked briefly at her children, but then she nodded.

"Best we get the bundles done ready, my lady."

"Aye," she said. "But what if snow come?"

"Then we'll be from here and make snug some'eres else. We mun move ahead o' snow, that's certain."

Will felt a stir of excitement, as though his courage had come to life. The thought of moving on filled him with a curious satisfaction. He was one of a travelling family and travel seemed the right thing.

Sim decided they should leave on Sunday morning, at the very time that Widow Tester was changing her name to Goody Penfold. They would then be well down the road, Sim claimed, and covered by the early dark, before any became aware of their going. They would make for that little scrubby wood where Star had been born, and where their cover was easily stretched among the sapling birches to make good shelter. There, too, was a small pit dug that held a store of nuts and dried mushrooms. They had four loaves which they had hoarded through the week. Rabbit and pigeon would be easily taken in this weather, though there could not be much meat on them.

They waited until everyone was in church and then set out, each carrying a burden but stepping easily on the hard ground. The frost had ironed away the worst ruts. Fairlight led the goats, but Delphi ran close by Will. Like him, she was excited by setting out. He took her hand and they walked together, pleased with one another's company.

They saw no one on the road. The sun shone. The ground maintained its hardness, like the iron that could be found within it. The birds were silent, ruffled and deceptively plump on the branches. Far ahead, on the clear distance, swelled the downs that stood protective against the sea.

Now Delphi took the goats and Fairlight ran to walk by Will and he took her hand in turn. The difference struck him for the first time – Delphi's hand was firm and sure, it stayed warm in his as they clasped one another. But Fairlight forever fidgeted her fingers and her palm was damp and clinging.

She laughed up at him, excited and feverish.

"Reckon that John Penfold holler sore when he come to the barn – eh, Willow? Naun left to be chased away!"

"Hush," he said, not knowing quite why, except that her manner made him uneasy.

Now Sim walked by Will and the two girls joined their mother.

"Best we get as near the town as maybe," Sim said. He seemed to invite some reassurance. "Truly, could be more passing on the road – but we needs think of your brother." He waited for Will to answer, but he only nodded. "There's a broken down cove I can recall, Will – not far from that place we'll rest soon – the place Star was born. That could be shelter till spring. Then there'll be brooms for the selling. Come spring there's not a housewife living but seeks after a new broom."

He sounded now quite confident and cheerful, but his tone had still some hidden doubt in it – as if he spoke for his own reassurance but needed more from Will. But just as Will had experienced, at that place, the certainty of not being alone, so now his father's words sounded a note of warning. He was touched, unreasonably, by a sudden acute fear ...

At dusk they came to the little wood and crept into its shelter. The birch saplings stood so close they were like a screen unfolded between this hiding place and the road they had just travelled. Soon the fire was burning, the true dark had come. They moved close together and made their supper of bread with a smear of honey. The goats bleated in a bewildered way. After a bit, Moll brought them closer to the fire and they settled, their warmth adding to the rest. The sky was clear above them and crowded with stars.

Will tried counting the stars as he lay, wrapped up in his cloak and warm enough yet sleepless. The silence was at once beautiful and threatening. It made him strain his ears for any sound. The cold kept the mice in their holes and so the owls were quiet ... Then he thought he heard a rhythmical sound and he sat upright, listening even harder.

At first he thought it was his own heartbeat that he heard so clearly ... Then he realised that the sound was growing louder.

Will put out his hand and shook Delphi gently.

She turned. "What ...?" She yawned.

"Listen. Someone's riding."

"Going's too hard." She yawned again and was ready to turn back to sleep. Then she checked and sat upright and shifted nearer to him. They sat listening. Will glanced quickly at Sim, but he was heavily asleep, released from the stricture of the barn's roof and walls.

"Come to the edge o' the wood, Delphi."

They crawled there, accustomed, like young animals, to moving soundlessly.

Now the hoofbeat was very clear, the air rang with the rhythm. Sometimes that rhythm broke and they knew the horse had stumbled. As the sound increased,

Sim woke and came to them. Again the horse stumbled and now it was possible to hear the rider shout out, angrily, "Keep up, you clumsy beast!"

Now indeed Will's blood ran as cold as the rime on the branches. Sim heard what he heard, and he pressed his two youngsters closer against the dark ground.

The rider passed. The sound of his going grew less, then sharpened again as he reached that ancient road that ran, so it was said, all the way back to London. Then there was silence as the road took a curve.

Sim let out a long breath. "There. Good he gone well away."

"John Penfold . . ." Will said, hardly daring to use his voice.

"Gone. Get back to your sleep. See not to rouse the others."

But Moll was already awake. She looked at Sim sharply, but seeing less in his face than she expected, turned to Will.

"Aye," she said, as though he had spoken. "I'll not forget that voice."

"He'm on his way," Sim insisted. "A-most to the town."

He lay down and was asleep instantly.

Moll beckoned Will. "Did y'see'm, Willow?"

"And heard him."

"What for should he ride out on his wedding night – even though he no lad and she no maid? Harm. He mean harm to us, my Willow. We need move from here by dawn."

☆

79

THERE was no sound of John Penfold's return that night. As soon as morning came they were packing up, stamping the fire. Star, who had been quiet while they were in the barn and had seemed almost to be thriving, now began again his long sad crying. Moll unpacked a bottle of a herb drink she sometimes gave him, and after he had drunk some of that he fell asleep. But something sorry seemed to have come upon him overnight. He had shrivelled again, he had wizened.

"He look like an elf," said Fairlight.

"Be silent!" her mother snapped.

Now Sim decided they had better not go to the place he had chosen, for it was too near to the road along which John Penfold had ridden.

"Better we get back into the forest," he decided.

Will had not heard before the cry of wretchedness and disappointment that Moll gave then.

"It's far – it's far, husband ..."

"Aye, so it is. And no cart to ride you in. But best for us all and let it be soon."

So they went, with far less determination than yesterday, down the ice-hard track towards that same old road that John Penfold had ridden in the night. He had headed south towards the town, but they would turn northward and so eventually find themselves back among forest ways.

The day was lightening. Frost hung thick and glittering on every twig, on every surface, streaking down the trunks of trees and patterning the smallest pond, prettifying the ice that sheeted the stream from shore to shore and tormenting the ducks who huddled hungry in the sad shelter of the bank. The high wide sky was colourless, cloudless and pure as the day moved across from the horizon. It seemed a morning for hope, so free it appeared, but there was little hope in the hearts of Sim Swayne, of Moll, of Will or Delphi. Even Fairlight dragged along, snivelling and scratching the backs of her cold hands.

The road was empty. None travelled and none lingered. All was silent, all was still.

Then a heron brought sudden movement, flapping in a huge arc, bound no doubt for the forest ponds that were big enough, and warm enough from cooling the iron, to resist the worst of the freezing and offer some fishing.

Instantly, just as stillness had gone, so silence, too, was banished. The road sent ahead the sound of hooves and the rumble of a cart.

On either side, the country lay clear in flat meadowland. There were few trees beside willows drawing the line of a stream. It seemed to Will that they must all of them stand out sharp and clear from one end of the great road to the other. There was nowhere, nowhere for even the smallest to hide.

7

JOHN PENFOLD's horse was as ugly as he was, and the two of them seemed set to out-do one another as they glared down at the travellers.

"Now see if you'll sneak into decent folks' barns!" Penfold shouted. "Now see what the law say to such as you – vagabonds – wastrels! Leeches sucking the livelihood of honest neighbours! I'll needs burn every stick of straw in my barn or ever I'll be rid of you!"

"It never were your barn till yesterd'y noon!" Moll shouted in her turn. "A good Christian soul like Widow Tester – she know well how to help the helpless!"

"I'll see you helpless!" Penfold bellowed – and he leant from the saddle and struck her across the face with his riding whip.

Had John Penfold been there alone, Sim could have found a way to punish him – but there were others with him. There was the constable, for one, seated in the cart, and a couple of men of the Watch; and a clerkly fellow who flourished a great paper. Sim was grabbed before he could spring, and it was Will who leapt at Penfold, as once before he had leapt to defend his father. He caught John Penfold round the thigh and hung on so furiously that the rider almost tumbled from his saddle.

"Pick off this young leech!" Penfold roared, hitting out vainly at Will. "Squeeze the blood out of him, the parasite!"

And Will was seized in his turn and struck and cuffed and held by one arm and lifted off the ground.

"Leave him!" Moll screamed. "Let be! Let be!"

She was Queen of the Pharisees but none heeded her command. The fellow with the paper began reading from it in a dreary, thin voice ... That here were vagabonds taken in all their guilt – that vagrancy was a crime under the law requiring due and just punishment – that they should be taken to the town and held in gaol there till the justices sat in court and could pronounce on their crime ... And therefore, God Save the King.

Now Sim was shoved into the cart and the others bundled in after him. Will still struggled so violently that one of the men gave him a great buffet about the head that sent him staggering, his ears ringing, his eyes filled with blood. Someone then heaved him over the cartside and he fell heavily into the bottom, knocking over Fairlight as he went.

Then the various officers of the law, including the constable but not the clerk, gathered up all the bundles and threw them clattering into the ditch. At which the goats ran here and there, bleating in terror.

"Those are mine!" Penfold cried. "I'll have those home where they belong."

Delphi, pale and shocked into silence, now began to cry wildly, and since Fairlight was already sick with terror and clinging to Moll, shaking and shivering and rubbing her forehead which had struck against the side of the cart when Will knocked her over, the scene could hardly have been more dismal.

"Well," said Penfold, eyeing the cartful with satisfaction, "I'll say thank-ye and take my way. Tell my brother I expect him to deal fairly."

"Aye, sir. He'll be told what you say, master."

"Good day, then."

"And good day to 'ee also, Master Penfold."

When the rider was out of earshot, someone laughed. When he was all but out of sight, the lesser of them scrambled into the ditch and opened the bundles, sharing out the spoils – such as they were.

Only one thing remained that belonged. Sim had kept hold of his stick, and now it clattered to the bottom of the cart as his hands were tied by the constable. Will slid himself over it, protecting it, at least for the present. As the cart began to move, he lay very still, his ears still buzzing, his limbs aching, his teeth gritted. "My brother", John Penfold had said. What brother? Could there indeed be a second Penfold as awful as the first ...?

☆

THE courthouse was a handsome building facing on to the town market place, and that was by the crossroads halfway up the hill. They had been hustled from the cart and shoved into a dim little room, where the clerk, whose name was revealed as Silas Titmuss, sat down ponderously at a high desk and began questioning them. Where were they from? Where were they going? Why were they going? Where had they spent the previous night? Did they know the penalty that might be meted out to vagabonds?

No one answered. Then Delphi whispered to Will, her voice shaking, "What shall happen to us, Willow?"

"Ah, now," said the clerk, pointing his quill pen at her and glaring over the desktop. "That's a wise question that's well asked. There's many things can happen to such as you are — like whippings and hangings."

Delphi sobbed and buried her head against Will's shoulder, and Fairlight clutched at Moll.

"Keep your threats to yourself," Sim growled. "What need to frit the little maid?"

"Best to look at the worst," the man said cheerfully. "It was Master John Penfold did indict you, and 'tis Master Robert, his brother, that is clerk to the justices, shall make the charge. So it's a family matter, you might say."

Then he closed his great book and wiped his pen on his sleeve and left the room, saying to the two men who guarded the door,

"Tell Ben Ashe he has fresh charges."

Then there was only one man left and he stayed silent, and so did all the rest. Then Star began to cry. Moll tried all she knew to quiet him, but the crying persisted, thin and nagging, an ugly, despairing sound.

Moll said to the man by the door, forced to be humble now, "The babby cry for milk."

The man laughed. "That's for you to offer'm!"

Moll bowed her head. In a small sad voice she said, "Then he mun die."

The man glanced at poor Star and said harshly,

"What shall you g' me for milk?"

Will watched his mother and saw her tremble. Hidden in her bodice still was the golden guinea. To part with that was to part with everything — to admit possession of such a thing was, as Sim had seen at once, to invite a charge of thieving. There was one other thing that might be bartered — Will still held on to the stick with its carved antler head.

Sim said quietly, "Gi'm the stick, Will."

"That's a weapon, anyhows," the man said, "and naun such shall be kept by any prisoner. But gi' it here to me and I'll fetch milk."

They watched him leave, calling to another of his fellows to take his place. But before he could do so, there came Ben Ashe, who was the prison turnkey. And in witness of his occupation there jangled at his belt a great bunch of keys big and small, the symbols of his power.

"Well some's fortunate and others not," he told Sim, as he shoved him ahead down the cold stone-walled passageway, the rest following miserably. "The justices has been sitting these several hour, but are now risen up and shall sit again this afternoon. A day later and you'd'a bin waiting here in this place till the next sitting – and that's beyond Epiphany. And had you come in here to answer your crimes at Michaelmas, when the sitting should'a bin – then you'd have found all here down-stricken wi' the plague." He laughed heartily, taking the bunch of keys from its hook and swinging it, so that keys jangled almost in tune to his babble of talk. "That save their Lordships a deal o' tedious judging, you might say. So now, sitting so late in the year, their work is much cut off." Again he laughed, again he swung his keys, and rattled them close to Delphi's ear. "So long's the snow keep up – they'll find time to deal wi' you."

"The snow –?" Moll muttered.

"These is rather of the lesser sort of gentlemen that sits this session – and have no town house so must travel home or pay lodging at the inn. And if the snow catch 'em – their pockets do suffer ... And here," he ran on without any change of tone, "is the parting place."

He shoved Sim to the right and Will after him, clanging and locking with a neat twist of the wrist a high barred door. Then with a terrible mock bow to Moll, he pushed her off to the left, the girls stumbling after, and as neatly and gracefully clanged and locked a second door.

THE gaol was below the court house and it was dank and drear and full of a terrible stench as any such place must be. It was lit and aired by a row of half-moon gratings and the prisoners could watch the feet and ankles, the hems and boots of the world going by. As the prisoners looked up and out at this display, so they could be looked in and down upon by louts and lads of the meaner sort who shouted abuse and mockery, hurled filth and rubbish through the bars and spat down into the dirty straw that covered the floor. Here were held those whose villainy of one sort or another had brought about their arrest, and here they must wait for the justices to sit. And, as Ben Ashe, the turnkey, had explained, if there should not be a sitting for weeks to come, then for weeks they must remain imprisoned.

For a moment or two after Ben Ashe had locked the door, Will dared not look around him. There was little light, in any case, and maybe it would have been better had there been less. For gradually Will's eyes accustomed themselves to the gloom and then he could see the worst that had befallen him. There were three other men and a boy in the narrow chamber, and the boy was confined in a cell with bars, while the men wore chains of one kind or another that rattled hideously whenever they moved. The boy added to the noise by walking round and round what amounted to a cage, banging his shoulder against the bars every few paces. Though Sim's wrists had been tied when they were all together in the cart, his hands were now free, so his case was better than the others.

The chains that bound Sim were chains of despair. He leant against the wall and beat his head against it so violently that Will half expected him to drop to the ground. He watched him almost with terror as he went next to the barred door and grasped the bars and peered and squinted towards the far door through which the others had vanished. His gaze was so intent, so piercing that Will almost believed his father had the power to see through bars and walls to where Moll and her other children endured their own miseries.

Will crept close to Sim. "Let be, master," he said in a soft, anxious whisper. "Maybe soon we'll see'em. We'll all be stood afore the justices – allus together."

Sim groaned and shoved at the bars as if to bend them.

"Where's him that was to bring milk? What happened to my fine walking-staff? He cheat us!"

Just then there was a hustle along the passage, and a woman's voice, very shrill and loud, crying.

"Give that to me, you lout. There's no man going visiting my prisoners, that's certain. Give it here!"

Then a tough, tubby little woman, with her hair hanging all about her face, and wearing a filthy torn apron of sacking, went banging along to the woman's door. She, like Ben Ashe, had a great bunch of keys. She chose one and opened the door. She went inside, shouting as she went,

"Where's the new prisoner? Stand up and show yourself, you wretch. Here's milk come for your little 'un. Think lucky there's soft hearts in hard places."

This drove Sim mad, and he rattled and banged more than ever, and shouted out,

"Moll, Moll! Call to me that you're still living! Call out, Moll – call out!"

Will saw his mother stand at the door, behind the bars. It was too dim to see her face, but she answered Sim in her own way, singing out to him in her fairy voice, telling him without words what only he would be able to understand. Then she moved away out of sight.

"What she tell, master?" Will asked, holding Sim's hands and trembling.

Sim let out a long sigh. "She say to hope, Willow. She say we'll be together again, and not long to wait."

Before Will could take this in, there was a great commotion in the women's prison, shouting and screaming and cries – Will thought he heard Delphi's voice. Then the little woman with the keys dashed out, crying loudly in her turn.

"Ben! Ben Ashe! Husband! Come here – come quick! There's one on 'em fell down and died!"

Behind Will and Sim as they stood by the door, the other men began to shout out, and the wild-eyed boy stamped his feet and rattled at the bars. Ben Ashe came running, his keys beating together, clanking like some awful cracked bell.

"What now, Betsy? Can't you keep 'em orderly?

Then starve 'em, I say!"

"I tell you – she fell and died!"

"Who fell and died?"

"Who else but the old witch woman?"

There was more bellowing as Ben Ashe shouted for Jem, for Dan, for Dick and Hal. A couple of them came running, and the old woman who had died was dragged out and carried away.

"What come to her?" Will asked, puzzled and disturbed by the quick brutality of it all. He had caught one quick glimpse of her face as she was carried past. "She look happy."

One, of the other men in the cell let out a guffaw.

"So might she! She's a sly old one, if ever there was. Fed and housed in this fine palace for all the long months – and at the town's expense – nursed through a fit of the plague, what's more – and got clean away just when her true reckoning should'a been made."

"What had she done?"

"Witchcraft, that's what. And bewitched her own death, b'the look of it. The mortacious old cheat!"

Then the turnkey was back and entering very purposefully. He called to the man who had just spoken and then kicked him to his feet and unlocked the chain round his waist that secured him to a ring in the wall. Then two of his men returned from carrying away the old woman, and between them they pulled the wild boy from his cage and carted him away struggling.

"Where he go?" Will asked in a whisper.

"It's two hour past noon," Ben Ashe told him, "and the justices is back at the Bench. Fine victuals changed many a prisoner's sentence, that I do know."

He was gone then in the wake of the hullabaloo made

by the boy and his fellow prisoner. Then all was silent. No one spoke and no sound of any movement could be heard, for thick floors and walls cut off the cells from the rest of the building. The prisoners did not return and the silence somehow grew deeper and colder. Will would have given much to hear Star crying.

Then again there was the sound of the jangling keys and Ben Ashe and his wife Betsy came hurrying.

"Your turn come next – what did I tell you?"

"Where are the others?" Will asked. "The other boy ..."

"Them? Well on their way b'now, I'd say. There's few hangings takes much time ... Now, sir and my lady – and maids and lads – follow me and we'll be rid o' the lot in an hour or less. Their worships is set to get home b'dusk."

☆

IN THE courtroom the justices sat at their long bench, conversing rather slowly together between cases. Although the turnkey had dismissed them as being lesser gentry, they still looked alarming enough to the prisoners. Maybe there was no actual lord among them today, but the rest were at the least solid, wealthy landowners, at the best knights of the shire – and all were there to perform their civic duties.

A number of more modest men, hatless, were gathered at one side of the court, and these were witnesses or guarantors of one sort or another. The prisoners were herded into a form of pen on the floor of the court, and around and behind them stood a cluster of townsfolk come to gape at the solemn proceedings and, if they were allowed the chance, to applaud or deride the sentences.

"Proceed with the next hearing," said a large gentle-man with a well-fed look. He sat in the centre of the rest and was clearly in charge of proceedings.

Will was standing with Delphi clutching one hand and Fairlight the other. Moll stood behind them, Star quite silent in her arms. Sim, for some reason unex-plained, was held apart from them, a rough-looking guard on either side. Will fixed his gaze on his father, trying to appear bold and strong-hearted, but trembling with a terrible dread of what was to happen. He was not helped by what he saw in Sim's face – despair had given way to a sullenness that could not help him or any of them.

The justice's clerk rose and bowed to the Bench. He held a long paper in his hand – but he was not the little inferior man who had read the charge to Sim and his family when they were taken on the road. This was a man far more formidable. He was in fact John Penfold's powerful brother, Robert, as became immediately clear.

"Make some haste, Master Penfold," the chief justice urged. "Time is short."

"The charge is one of vagrancy, your worship," the clerk announced. "The accused did take possession unlawfully of a good barn full of straw, that is the property of a respectable yeoman, and, having no dwelling place did make it their home and would not be put out. Also, there is evidence of theft of livestock and other commodities – as gowns, shoes, bonnets – whose whereabouts may not now be discovered . . ."

Will began to lose track of the business – of the clerk's droning, of the justices' questions. Sometimes he was just aware that Moll had been questioned, and had answered. Around him he heard the townsfolk shuffling and stamping their feet to keep warm, and sometimes muttering among themselves, and even sometimes crying self-righteously – "Aye – aye! His worship speak true ..." and so on. Now his trembling had ceased, but only because he was numb with fear. The two girls still clung to him but his hands had grown limp and he was ready to fall to the ground. He feared bitterly for his father. Why was he held apart? Will thought with terror of the walking staff with its carved head; he thought of the golden guinea.

Now there was more noise than there had been. Will tried to rouse himself. Moll had just answered a question and something about it had angered Sim. He began to shout out, a contradiction, perhaps – Will had lost the thread of the business and was utterly confused.

"Remove that man," the chief justice ordered.

"Shall he not be sentenced, your worship?" the clerk asked, rather sharply.

"The delay is his own. There will not be time this sessions. Take him away."

There was instantly much arguing among the crowd, as Sim was dragged away still shouting. The clerk again bellowed for silence. Her head drooping against Will's, Moll gave a wretched, groaning cry.

"We shall now deliberate," the chief justice announced. "The case is a straightforward one, but there is an item that needs thought. The law in regard to vagrants and vagabonds has been recently amended."

He then turned to his neighbour and spoke in his ear and others turned to one another, nodding or shaking their heads, very solemn and deliberate. Sometimes it seemed the matter was settled, and then that it never could be. The onlookers grew impatient. A huge book on the Bench was opened, consulted, passed up and down. And after that, heads were nodded, the book was handed to the clerk.

"Read the final words of the act to the accused," he was ordered.

The court was silenced. The clerk read at a great roaring gabble so that barely a word could be recognised.

Moll whispered frantically to Will, "What he say? What shall it do for us?"

Now Will was indeed roused. The removal of Sim had been had enough, but now he saw that his mother must be punished for what she did not understand. There was none to speak for her, for all of them. He felt his mother shaking with terror. What magic was left in her to face these mysterious happenings? Was it such wickedness to accept shelter in Widow Tester's barn? They had done no harm to it ... Could it be the matter of the goats – the dues unpaid to the lord of the manor ...?

"Have you understood?" The chief of the justices was, patiently enough, addressing himself directly to Moll.

She shook her head, her eyes blacker than ever with her misery.

"Listen, then, and I shall tell you in simple words. The law now proclaims thus: That any taken up for vagrancy shall be returned to his own parish, there to be dealt with as those in charge may see fit."

He stared hard at Moll, but it was not a harsh or

cruel stare and Will's spirits lifted slightly. It sounded as though matters might not be as hard as expected.

"Which is your parish, woman?" the justice asked, patiently still.

Moll frowned and stared. The clerk then repeated the question.

"I've naun," she said.

"Come now – no parish? We must all be born in one place or another."

Moll began to speak in a low, frightened voice. The clerk tried to stop her but was rebuked from the Bench.

"Let her speak. Let her tell her tale. Only, for pity, let her speak briefly."

"Sir –" began Moll.

"Your worship," corrected the clerk.

"Your worship, my husband, Sim Swayne, do ply a tinker's trade. He did ever work honest. He had his cart and tools to prove his trade – but one day they was stole away from us, and the old horse along wi' the rest. And so we come at last to Widow Tester, who give leave we shall lie in the barn till winter's gone."

The clerk at this rose and whispered something to the Bench.

"I see – I see," his worship murmured. He frowned a little as he looked down at Moll. "I am told this good woman no longer holds the barn. You cannot, therefore, claim her consent."

"Aye," cried Moll, "and why she hold it no more is no more'n because her new husband seize it! Do you ask him," she cried, pointing at the clerk, Robert Penfold, "ask him who hold it now!"

There was now some fidgeting among the members of the Bench, for all this, in their opinion, was taking far too long. The justice in charge saw this and was quick to act. His manner sharpened and he frowned impatiently.

"Well, well — let that be. It has little bearing on the case, as things stand. The outcome is clear enough. The law commands that you shall be returned to your place of origin by the officers of this court, and you will not roam again beyond your parish boundary on peril of being committed to prison." He was already gathering his papers together, preparing to rise. "And your husband must go back to his birthplace, if it is a different one, and where, I ask, were your children born — for they belong nowhere but in their own parishes. And indeed, since you are wanderers by choice, so let you pay the price of it. The Bench will now rise. The court is dismissed."

8

ALONGSIDE the courtroom was a small chamber, very dusky, with one miserable lamp standing on a bare table. At the table, with quill and ink and paper, sat Robert Penfold and his assistant, the little long-nosed man who had taken part in their arrest. Before them, as if yet again on trial, stood the Queen of the Pharisees and her children.

"I misremember," she said.

Robert Penfold slapped down his pen, rose to his feet and crying to his assistant, "Do what you will — but let it be soon done!" he hurled himself from the room.

"The church, now," said Silas Titmuss. "You shall remember the name of the church or the worst must happen. Where were you baptised? Which church?"

He did not say what the worst might be, but Moll hesitated. Will could not imagine how anyone could remember such distant matters, and in any case not one of them, as Widow Tester knew, had been baptised. But he knew, and Delphi knew, too, that Moll supposed she saw an escape.

"St Wildered's," she said.

"St Wilfred's — Wilfred's," snapped Titmuss. He began at once to write. "That'll be over East Brambleford," he said in a satisfied way. Master Robert would be pleased with him. "Now, now — see how we're progressing," he said, more to himself than to anyone else. "And the boy?"

"St George," lied Moll.

"St George. That's Sellingham by Marshtide. Good.

And the girls?"

Moll hesitated. She looked at Will in a hunted, haunted way. Perhaps it was only then that she saw what, in her flurry and fear, she had done to them all. She put her hand over her eyes and gave a great sob.

"St Bride's," she whispered. "Both."

"Little Mintingstead," wrote Titmuss. "Very good. This shall be a fine riddance and none better pleased by it than Master Robert Penfold. Unless," he said, with a snigger, "it be his brother, Master John!"

Moll bent her head over the poor quiet bundle that was Star and was silent.

"There now, there now," said Titmuss with great benevolence. "You shall keep the babe for yourself."

Will spoke for the first time. He was the only man among these women and his responsibilities fell hard across his shoulders, as hard and heavy as that wooden yoke that was lost to them now.

"Where we go till leaving, master? Shall it be prison agin till we leave?"

Titmuss looked at Will. His glance was shrewd and clever.

"Not so, my smart young sir. There are those below that you shall not plot with. Here's where you are and here's where you shall remain."

Moll roused herself with difficulty. "My husband. When'll I have a word wi' him?"

Titmuss laughed. "Why – you have bid him farewell. Did you not call after him when he left the court? Was not that your goodbye? So we all supposed."

"What shall come to him? He'll die in that place! He'll die!"

"Aye, so it may well be. In that place or maybe just outside it." He shook his head as if in sympathy. "Come next sessions I doubt but we'll have his lordship on the Bench. He's a hard man and much in favour of hanging."

This time Moll did not cry out, but said in a strange voice her children hardly recognised.

"Take this – and let me get to him."

And across the table she slid the golden guinea that Delphi had found shining in that place where they had been happy, yet where all their troubles had begun.

Titmuss was still. He looked at the coin and he looked at Moll. Then slowly he picked up the guinea, turned it this way and that, balanced it on his palm, closed his fingers on it and rose. He took the key from the lock, and as he did so he slipped the coin into his pocket. Without looking back, he left the room, pulling the door after him. Then he fitted the key into the lock again and turned it. It was a big lock and a big key. It clattered as the gates of hell must clatter when they close.

"He'll be back," Moll said to her children. "He'll be back and bring your father."

But it was dawn before the key turned again, and it was Ben Ashe who stood there, shouting to them to get out into the yard.

☆

EVEN at this hour, with the light barely lifting the night away, Will saw the day's weather in his mind's eye. It would be cloudless, the sun showing red from rise to set, the frost persisting, renewing, tightening a grip already strong and bitter. But there was far more than weather about this day. Life as Will had known it was about to be carved into pieces.

There was a pump in the yard which, as it was bound round with straw, still gushed.

"Wash your faces," Moll ordered her children. "Drink while you may. We none on us know where the next chance come from."

They were too chilled in body, too stunned in mind to answer her. Fairlight clung to Delphi and Delphi, her face like chalk, looked from her mother to Will and back again but saw no comfort. When they had washed in the icy water and drunk what they could from their cupped hands, Moll, holding Star in one arm, held out the other and the three of them went and pressed close against her.

"You know what's to be? You heard the words that was spoke agin us. We must all be set upon our ways. And where they shall be, I cannot tell – for I said the first that came into my head. So we'll get driv to some crossroads and there get parted. And may I be cursed for it – I made the fault. I did think to make it too hard for 'em, but only made it easy. Whyn't I say we was all come from one place? Why'd I get so trapped and vlothered?"

"Star done the best on us," Will said in a low voice. "There'll be but one by day's end of all the Queen of the Pharisees' children ..."

Moll flung back her head and they shrank back, fearing to hear again her cry of terrible despair. But she checked herself and instead smiled a little.

"Your father call me that. Sim Swayne call me that."

"What shall come to him?" Will asked, still in that barely-heard voice. "Shall they ... Shall he ...?"

Maybe we'll naun see'm agin, my Willow ... Maybe ..."

"There was the gold guinea, Mam."

"Aye. Once there was."

At this point, Ben Ashe appeared and handed them some crusts and a stringy bit of meat.

"Eat sharp," he ordered. "The clerk's here to see you on your way."

Moll made one last bid. "My husband – there were a promise I should speak to'm ...."

Ashe laughed, and at that moment there was a wheel rumble and a cart was driven to the gateway.

"Bring your bread wi' you," Ashe said, shoving them impatiently towards the little postern gate that stood open. "Carts is handy and can't be long away."

They went outside on to the slippery cobbles where the cart waited, drawn by a big bony horse with dismal ears. There were three men besides the driver and they leant against the cart, yawning and spitting, blowing on their hands.

Now Moll wept in silence, her tears dropping almost to the ground, but her children were too stunned to weep with her, or to know how to comfort her and one another.

"The sooner started, the sooner done," Ben Ashe cried. "Leave lolling there, Jem. Dan – give'm a hand. Get the lot on 'em on their way."

Then there came a scuffle and a struggle, as Will suddenly roused himself and struck out at Dan as he seized Moll round the waist. Everyone began shouting and the two girls screamed wildly, their feet slipping

on the ice-covered cobbles as they strove to escape
. . .

A rider coming to the courthouse dismounted as if
he had business there. He tethered his horse to a
hitching post, but then paused before entering the
building. He glanced with distaste towards the noise.
He hesitated and then moved in that direction. He
was a man of middle years, middle height. His dark
clothes suggested a sober turn – perhaps he was a
schoolmaster, a parson, a man of learning. Though
his face was not handsome its expression was both
strong and gentle.

"Let be – let be!" he cried to Jem, who had grabbed
Fairlight and seemed ready to toss her into the cart
like a handful of hay. "So young a child – what can
she have done to be handled so roughly? Have some
care with her, friend. Young bones are easy broken."

At the sound of this human voice, Moll swung
round and would have cried out for help, whether or
not there could be such a thing in this dreadful place.
But Dan seeing what she would do, cuffed her hard,
so that she fell into the bottom of the cart and lay
there stunned. She dropped Star as she fell, but he
gave no cry. Will, already bundled into the cart along
with the girls, stooped to pick up his brother, but
Moll roused and snatched him close to her.

"Come now, come now . . ." the gentleman began,
clearly distressed.

At this moment, the clerk, Titmuss, came from the
courthouse.

"Mr Hazelgrove, sir," he said, bowing and looking
more awkward than merely surprised. "I did not look
to see you here today, sir. And so early."

"I am come in great haste to speak with Robert Penfold. Concerning the case of my parishioner – the old soul falsely accused of witchcraft."

"Falsely, sir?"

"Ay – falsely. For her neighbour who testified against her now confesses to bearing false witness. The justices sit today?"

"Why no – the sessions is concluded."

"Then – I am in time to save her?"

"I fear, rather, that you are too late. She died last night. It did seem her good fortune – seeing the charge."

Mr Hazelgrove stared at Titmuss and seemed stupefied by the news.

"What is this about? She survived the plague – and is she dead now?"

"She did on a sudden fall from her stool. She was dead sure enough. I suppose she had magicked her end!" And he laughed.

"God save us all," the gentleman said. "What had she to answer, poor wretch ... And these," he cried, nodding to the cart, "what have they done that must be punished?"

"Do not trouble yourself, sir. They are vagabonds and shall be sent where they belong."

"Children? Can children be named vagabonds?" He gave a snort of impatience and turned away. "Take me to Robert Penfold. I must learn more of the old woman."

"Jack!" called Titmuss to a man standing at the gate. "See Mr Halzelgrove indoors and call the justice's clerk to him. I have business here must not be delayed."

Even now, Jack at his elbow, Titmuss bowing a farewell, the gentleman hesitated. His face was full of an extraordinary compassion. It seemed, almost, that he positively shared the misery of these unknowns. Then, with a great sigh he turned away and followed Jack inside.

Relieved of this exasperating interruption, Titmuss proceeded to his task. He dragged a paper from his pocket and read through it at great speed, gabbling and fumbling.

"You understand?" he concluded. "This is signed by three justices – no felon could ask more." He stared at their blank faces. "Simpletons! It orders you shall be driven to the crossroads and there set on your several ways, each to his own parish and the churchwardens there of. That's plain enough for any. Dan – let you take the boy – Jem, see the girls safe to the end of their road. Tom – let me wish you joy of the mother. See you don' leave her roaming. I know her sort. She'll be back on this doorstep soon's we can turn round."

"That's a long doddle on a cold day," Jem grumbled.

"It's a doddle must be concluded, however. Here, Dan – it's all written down. You tell me lately you're a reading man. Now get off with you and never let me see your dirty faces more till the task's done."

Will slumped down in the straw and put his hands over his eyes. He could not bear to look at his mother and sisters, for Moll's utter misery seemed spread over them like some dreadful blight. As the cart moved off, all were silent, not knowing or caring which way they went. The sun was now up but remained a crimson disc in the colourless sky. Fields stretched frost-white and trees stood rigid. Seabirds had come up river and wheeled and wailed over the barren countryside. In the cart, no one murmured, not Moll or her grown children, not Star, not any one of the sullen men. Only the driver whistled through his teeth as the horse plodded drearily near and nearer to the moment of parting.

☆

LONG before the promised crossroads, the cart drew up by a track that slanted off to their left in a north-westerly direction.

"Out, then, and smart about it," Jem ordered Will. "There's no good sense in slow parting. The swifter the sooner, as 'tis said of a knife cut."

Moll wrapped her arms round Will and held him as though she would somehow mould him into herself and so keep him forever. Delphi and Fairlight hung about his waist. No one spoke or shed a tear until Moll straightened her shoulders and pushed Will away.

"Never forget," she said then. "Never, never, my Willow. Think on me and on Sim Swayne, your good father and master. Think on them forest days that was so free. One day we come together again, surelye – though we need to die first."

Dan shouted for haste, then, and Moll again shoved Will from her. Will hugged Fairlight and then so clung to Delphi that she cried. Then he stooped down to Star, where Moll had laid him in the straw.

"Nay – let be," Moll said softly. "Leave him lie, the sad mawkin."

Will turned away at once and climbed from the cart. He knew that his only brother was dead and safe.

Dan grabbed Will by the arm. The driver shook up the horse. The wheels crunched over the frost. As the cart moved, so Dan pulled Will towards the new track. Then Moll called. It was not a call in her woman's voice but a fairy call that seemed to drag Will back to her. Dan must have heard that much, for he tightened his grip and began to hustle Will away. Dan looked pale, for the cry had been so unearthly and forlorn it had almost made him drop his charge and rush into hiding.

"What woman's that?" he muttered. "What woman's that, boy – that call herself your mother?"

"She'm Queen o' the Pharisees," Will answered, only he did not speak the words aloud. Resisting Dan's hold on his arm, he hung back, watching the cart moving on its way until it was snatched from him by sprawling hedge and undergrowth. For a time he still heard the wheel-rumble, the clop of the horse, so hard was the ground and so clear the air. Then all was quiet. Only his own footfall and Dan's more clumping step broke the winter silence.

In Will's mind there was a silence, too. He could not remember where he was going, or the names of the parishes to which his mother and sisters had been sent. This was the worst silence of all, thickening and deepening as he struggled to recall the names that had been spoken just once by Silas Titmuss, as they stood before him in that chilly ill-lit chamber and tried to understand what had happened to them . . .

This terrible silence, which seemed as though it

might never shatter, gave way gradually to the sound of a traveller on the road. There was a single rider coming this way. He trotted cautiously and sedately yet made a good steady progress along the way that Dan was unwillingly tramping with Will. The sound roused Will, brought him out of his chilled unhappiness and filled him instead with a dream full of hope and salvation. He saw again in his eager mind's eye, the expression on the face of Mr Hazelgrove as he heard news of the old woman, as he looked towards Moll and her children; towards Will.

Now the rider was nearer. He was bound to overtake them, for they had passed no lane or track to right or left that could have carried him away. The sound of hooves increased. It was only with difficulty that Will forced himself to look back, for he dreaded to be disappointed. What sun there was shone behind the rider and it was impossible to see anything but a black shape. But surely his hat, the way it sat on this head, his cloak, the way it flowed from his shoulders, seen even in this undefined way, did suggest the very man – Mr Hazelgrove himself, who seemed no stranger but the only friend Will might hope to find in all the world.

Peering over his shoulder, straining to see, Will almost fell head-long. Dan grabbed his arm.

"Keep they feet up. Stop doddling and tripping. Turn a foot and break an ancliff-bone and I'll leave 'ee to rot."

The rider was a stone's throw behind; the rider was level. Will looked up. The dream became reality.

"Dan! It's Mr Hazelgrove!"

And as the trotting horse overtook and passed

them, Will jerked away from Dan and broke into a run that would keep him level with the rider's stirrup.

☆

MR HAZELGROVE shouted a warning.

"Keep clear of the hooves, boy! I'll not guarantee my horse if you tease him."

"Master!" called Will. "Master!" And because he was losing breath and was weak from having had so little to eat, the word was jerked out of him.

Mr Hazelgrove reined to a walk, then halted. He sat with one hand on the horse's neck. He looked down at Will, frowning slightly.

Dan, who had been left behind, now came roaring up and struck at Will in fury.

"Young devil! Demon, you! See what you'll get when you run from me!"

He struck again, with better force, and Will was knocked to the ground.

"Ah – I know you now," Mr Hazelgrove said. "Are you not one of those men I saw outside the court-house? And this boy – is he not one of that pitiful family?"

"So he is – and a young brute, as you see. And I'm under orders to get him to his own parish and see he is put into the churchwardens' hands. And let 'em see to put the fear o' God into him, I say."

"What parish? You are set for Sellingham by Marshtide."

"I'm glad to hear it, your honour. And not many more mile on, I'd hope."

"Eleven, I should say, from hereabouts."

Dan groaned and kicked out at Will, who was now

108

picking himself up. "Curse and be damned to him that drags me these miles! Let him die in a ditch for making my feet ache!"

"Be silent!" Mr Hazelgrove said sharply. "Respect my cloth if not your own sad soul. Sellingham is my parish. I am its pastor. Leave the boy with me and get on your way. I'll see him safe to the right hands."

"Ah, sir – that'd be noble. But what'll Master Justices' Clerk Penfold have to say?"

"You may allow me to deal with that matter." Mr Hazelgrove fished in his pocket and flicked a coin towards Dan, who fell instantly on his knees to chase its rolling over the cold ground. "Take that and get off, you rogue. Your manner offends me."

Dan found the coin and scrambled to his feet. Without looking towards Mr Hazelgrove or Will, he made off fast down the narrow track.

☆

WILL stood staring up at Mr Hazelgrove. He was now very much afraid. He had longed for Mr Hazelgrove to appear, had imagined him as a saviour. Now, alone with him, Will knew he was even more of a stranger than the hateful Dan.

"Come now," the rider said. "It's not so far. See you keep at my stirrup – I shall do no more than walk."

He moved off at once. Will began to follow, dazed and chill. Though he only walked, the horse covered the ground very steadily, for he was a tall beast. Will ran beside him and the movement began to warm him. It also took his breath away. The ring of the hooves covered the sound of Will's gasping, but though he began to stumble, almost to reel, pride kept him upright. Mr Hazelgrove did not look round. It was though he had set Will a task and on its successful performance might depend all the future. In spite of this he was unable to keep up the pace. Pain stabbed at his side, the horse and its rider began to mist and dazzle. Will knew he must fall, and with what was left to him of breath and strength, he called out to Mr Hazelgrove.

It was as though his mother called for him, the cry was so strange. So strange, indeed, that Mr Hazelgrove turned at once and seeing the boy fall, turned back and dismounted. He knelt by Will, lifting his shoulders, all the time muttering in self-reproach.

"There now – I am a dull beast not to see thy state. Come child – take comfort ... Ah what a fool to see so little! May God forgive my stupidity – the poor soul's half starved and frozen ..."

He got Will to his feet and then urged him towards the horse.

"Catch hold when I joss you up – catch at the saddle. There now – wind your hands fast in Stamper's mane – he'll be patient. Now do you stay still and lean on me and we'll soon be homeward. Here, now – I'll tuck this end of my cloak round your shoulders."

The words came now in a tone of warmth and encouragement, wasting no more time on self-reproach ... Will was torn between respect for so solid a gentleman and a longing to sink back against his shoulder indeed and break into babyish tears. Between the two impulses, he held himself as stiff as a stone.

Mr Hazelgrove kicked Stamper to a trot. The track seemed to swallow itself behind them, and ahead to beckon them on. Riding perched ahead of this stranger, towards as strange a future, Will had no means, no skill, no imagination free enough to paint that future in any colour save black. The motion of the horse mingled with his own galloping thoughts. Rhythmic and heavy they bemused and lulled him. He fell back, then, against Mr Hazelgrove, as if against his own father, and slept.

9

IT WAS warm in the kitchen – warm as Will had never known warmth, with a great fire on the big hearth, burning bright and clear and smokeless. A cauldron of water stood heating to one side of the hearth, and hanging on the other was a closed pot that swung very slightly on its iron chain. From under the lid crept an odour so enticing it made Will quite faint and giddy. When he roused to find Mr Hazelgrove pulling him from the saddle, Will's first impulse as his feet touched the ground had been to bolt. He had made a quick dive under Mr Hazelgrove's arm but had been instantly checked. His arm held firmly, but certainly not roughly, he had been led into the kitchen of the parsonage, Mr Hazelgrove's solid square house that stood only a step from the church ... Now he waited, trembling and shivering in spite of the warmth, possessed by a piercing fear of what might happen next, and by longing for food. And as he stood there, five pairs of eyes surveyed him.

Besides Mr Hazelgrove there was his wife, who had been summoned to the kitchen. There was Dorothy and there was Peg, and they were young maidservants; and there was Leah, an older woman, who was doubtless responsible for whatever was stewing at the fire.

"Fetch the boy a stool, Peg," Mr Hazelgrove said.

"Aye – quick, Peg," said Leah. "He look near swimey to me."

"Sit down, boy," Mr Hazelgrove said. "No need to shake so. You are safe now."

"What am I to understand?" asked his wife, a pale woman, small with dark smooth hair showing from under her plain cap. "What have you been about this time, sir?"

"Why, here is a boy, as you see, wife – a poor boy in great need of succour. Are we not taught to care for such? And why should we not welcome a willing lad?"

"For sure – if he indeed be willing. You have not always proved right in such matters. And he looks a poor thing, indeed. What sort of strength may he have?" The lady grew increasingly vexed and seemed unable to stop talking. "And who is he? And how found? Have you picked him from the town gutter? Upon my word, Mr Hazelgrove, you should not be let ride to town alone! And, I must remind you, it was not for this you travelled through the cold – but to save poor Goody Yule."

"Alas," said Mr Hazelgrove, "she needed no saving, poor soul. She had gone to her Maker and there she shall find her solace."

These words, though softer spoken, reminded Will of the blind preacher, who spoke often of his Maker in bold and ringing tones. But whether spoken soft or spoken loud, they remained a puzzle to Will.

"Ah, poor Goody!" cried Mrs Hazelgrove. "So sadly and so badly done by. Did you not see her living?"

"She had died a few hours before. Maybe the boy can tell. Did you see her – an old woman, very frail and timid?"

Will answered, speaking for the first time since he came indoors, "She fell sudden off'n her stool and

113

were carried by, dead." He had never heard his voice so rough and croaking.

A cry came from Mr Hazelgrove's wife, and she retreated several paces, holding her hands as though to fend off disaster.

"But was she not shut up in the town gaol?" she cried. "Then how shall the boy have seen her save by being there himself? And is this so? Then what have you brought into my house?"

Now of the five pairs of eyes only two remained steady – Mr Hazelgrove's and Leah's. Of the three others, the mistress seemed ready to swoon in horror, while the maids twittered and gasped and eyed Will with the utmost hostility. He shrank as he sat there on the three-legged stool, trying to make himself smaller, even invisible.

"Is it so? Is it so? Speak truly, sir!" cried his wife.

"It is so," he agreed quietly. "He is a poor wanderer, homeless and lost, bereft of his parents. Shall he be punished for such faults?"

"That place is verminous – full of hideous disease. I asked had you picked him from the gutter – but this is far worse. He will not only shed sickness among us – he will steal our baubles and prey on the larder. Send him away! Turn him out! You said he was a wanderer – then pray let him wander!"

"Nay, that I cannot," Mr Hazelgrove said firmly, "for it would disgrace my calling ... Leah – let him be tubbed and his hair cut." Then he said to Will, as though he had only just thought about it, "You must tell me your name."

For a second or two, Will could not remember what he was called. Then he mumbled that he was

Will Swayne.

"Then, Will, I pray you give over shivering. Clothes – you need clothes. We shall soon see the difference when you stand up in good clothes."

There was such a silence then within the kitchen, where hams hung comfortably smoking by the chimney and bunches of drying herbs among the rafters, that Will stopped shivering for no better reason than that he was stiffened by fear.

"What clothes, husband?"

It seemed that Mr Hazelgrove had said something quite out-rageous for his wife had turned white then bright red and was clenching her hands together as if barely able to contain herself.

"My dear soul," said her husband gently, "you know well we have clothes of his size lying idle. May they not come to use again?" He smiled anxiously and tried to take her hand, but she drew back instantly. "Come now," he urged her, "take joy in a Christian deed. I know you have a generous heart."

"Our dead son's clothes for a filthy vagabond boy? Never! I'll burn 'em, rather!"

She turned and rushed away, letting the door slam behind her with a violence that made everyone start and wince.

Will stared at the ground, at the worn stone slabs of the kitchen floor, and he longed for what was to him the safety of grass and bracken, of mossy banks and rocky tracks. He remembered Dan's hard voice, spitting its way between blackened teeth, saying "The churchwardens shall know how to punish your villainy . . ." What would happen to him? Would they beat him? Would they shut him up tight and stuffy in some dark little room? The warm kitchen had seemed alarming enough but it was nothing compared with his imaginings. The truth would surely come out that he had no more been born in Mr Hazelgrove's parish than among the clatter and bustle of London town itself ... What then?

Will looked wildly around, ready to run – but Mr Hazelgrove stood between him and the door, while the windows were tight closed – it was no day to let the weather indoors.

"Leah," said Mr Hazelgrove, and he sounded weary, "pray see the boy well scrubbed. Find him a clean shirt at the very least."

Without waiting for her reply, he went after his wife.

Leah had been standing by the long table that was big enough for a score of men and maids to sit down to dinner. She moved to the hearth and put her hands on Will's shoulder. He looked up at her quickly, furtively, afraid of what he might see. She was not, perhaps, a laughing woman, but her face had a look of contentment and therefore her eyes were kind.

"No need to look so frit. There's naun'll harm thee in this household. All here are Christian souls. But washed you must be and shall be. There's water in the cauldron hot enough to cleanse the Devil himself." She called to the maids, "Dorothy, do you get down to Goody Tuppen and beg a shirt and breeches – her grandson's much of a size wi' this'un. The master shall see she do well of her kindness. Peg – fetch my shears and then bring the tub ... Did you say your name's Will, child?"

The word "child" put a bit of spirit back into him.

"I'm Will Swayne. Strong enough to do a man's work."

"Then stand like a man," said Leah, "till I cut off they filthy locks o' yourn ..."

She bore down on him, turning back her cuffs as she did so. Maybe the churchwardens would be better than what he must put up with now.

Will was accustomed to wear clothes little better than a scarecrow. The garments produced by Leah almost frightened him. They were so tidy, there was not a tear or a wear to be seen. And though they were the Sunday best of no more than a farmer's grandson, yet to Will they appeared the attire of a gentleman. How would he move easily in them? How keep them clean, as they seemed to deserve, from dawn to dusk? Shirt, breeches, a worsted doublet with sleeves, thick knitted stockings, shoes a good deal too big ... He imagined the laughter of Delphi and Fairlight, could they see him now. He thought of his mother and wondered if she would be proud or sorry at the change in his appearance. And his father? He might see nothing better than a lad "sprugged up and wi' a new master". Will sat by the fire as Leah had ordered him and gobbled down the bowlful of good thick gruel she had made him; but his thoughts were with Sim gulping rotten meat and mouldy bread in the town gaol. He put the bowl aside, for he could not swallow any more, and his own fortune in comparison filled him with guilt and with regret.

Leah watched him but said no word about the half empty bowl. She continued in silence about her own affairs. Will knew he must speak or she would not, but it was growing dusk before he found himself any

117

words. He heard himself saying, in a meek voice he hardly recognised,

"Where'll I be put now?"

"In the care of the churchwardens," said Leah, who was less of an easy comforter than Mr Hazelgrove. "It must be for you as the law say. 'Tis they churchwardens as have the law to carry out. You must be taken to 'em when the master say. Perhaps in the morning. They shall decide what must be done wi' you."

"What if I'll not go?" said Will, scowling.

"You know what comes to disobedient lads. They get sore beaten. The churchwardens is solid respectable men. They'll find you a master, one way t' other way – and he shall put you to work – and see you obey and do what he tell."

He said no more. His head drooped as he sat there in the warm and only pride helped him to swallow tears of lonely despair.

Outside there was change. A wind now blew and great clouds rolled to the north and east. Just as the last light went Mr Hazelgrove, wearing cloak and hat, returned from some errand and called out to one of the men as he crossed the yard to the house.

Leah peered from the window. "He look weary," she said. "He's never a man to let matters rest. He'll have been to the churchwardens, you mark me. He'll have that to tell you and'll send for you to the parlour, like as not."

What could that mean? What sort of word was *parlour*? Was it some place of punishment? Will knew nothing of what to expect in the house of a modest gentleman.

Sure enough, Dorothy came into the kitchen just then, and it was as Leah had said.

"The master call for ale, Leah. Shall I draw it, or you?" She looked at Will. "I'd niver've known'm! You're to come to the parlour wi' me. Soon's I've got the ale, I'll show the way."

Will followed her, stumbling a bit in his big shoes. The parlour now seemed formidable, for it must be there that Mr Hazelgrove would sit to drink his ale.

"Come in," he called to Will, as Dorothy took the tray and set it beside him and the boy hesitated in the doorway. "Come here. I have things to say to you."

Will had feared the presence of Mr Hazelgrove's unfriendly wife, but he sat alone. He was heating a poker in the fire and when he had poured his ale he plunged in the poker so that the liquid hissed and smoked. It seemed like sorcery, and Will jumped back.

Mr Hazelgrove looked up at him and very slightly chuckled.

"The ale is mulled," he said. "I have warmed it and so we may call it mulled." He drank and seemed satisfied with his work. Then he wiped his mouth on a long fine kerchief that he drew from his sleeve. Then he said, and now rather solemnly, "Did you not tell me your name is Will Swayne?"

Will nodded, unable to look anywhere but at Mr Hazelgrove's face – though there were things in the room so extraordinary, so beyond his imagining that he longed to stare and pry.

"And twelve years old, so you appear to me. Is that so?"

"My mam say that. Nigh on thirteen now."

119

"I have been at the parish records in my church, Will Swayne – which means that I have opened great books where are written the names of all here baptised or wed or buried since a little more than a hundred years. Do you understand?"

Will nodded again, since this was what Mr Hazelgrove seemed to require. He had certainly not dealt in such matters before, but he knew well enough what they must lead to.

"Will Swayne – I do not find your name among the parishioners of Sellingham. And do you understand that?"

This time Will neither nodded nor shook his head. He stared at Mr Hazelgrove and his fear must have been plain enough to see, for Mr Hazelgrove looked fussed and tut-tutted, saying, "Come, come – you need not look so. I am not accusing. Only try to tell me how this comes about?"

It was difficult. Will managed two or three words but they seemed to make little sense. He sought about for others but they fled away and left him empty headed.

"Did you stand before the Bench?" Mr Hazelgrove asked. "The justices, boy. In the court house."

"They say – go where we got born ... And Delphi was one place and Fairlight another ..."

Mr Hazelgrove was now the more bewildered. "Delphi? Fairlight? What are these?"

"My sisters."

"Ah." Mr Hazelgrove considered this, and then asked Will what had happened when the justices made their pronouncement. "Your mother was with you – I saw her myself. What did she answer?"

"I've forgot what she say . . ." What he had forgotten were the names of the churches she had so wildly claimed for her family's safe baptising. They were names he had never heard, as were the village names that had been seized upon and written down that the matter might have an end. "And nex'dy poor Star did die," he said as his thoughts ran on over the miserable end of his brother.

"Star –?"

"My brother."

Mr Hazelgrove did not immediately reply to this, digesting this third strange name with difficulty. But then he seemed to muster all his powers of patience and persuasion. He set about the rest of the business with the care and precision he would afford to any other weighty matter.

"Come now," he said. "Sit by me here and tell me all you know of yourself from your first remembering."

IT TOOK a long time. How to tell about the Queen of the Pharisees and about Sim Swayne? Will had not come by a great store of language, and some words he used were clearly unknown to Mr Hazelgrove – yet he must surely be a scholar. When Will said "We was maundering along the mavin", Mr Hazelgrove frowned and all but scratched his head. But then he grew thoughtful and careful, asking, "Is that word the same as *wandering*? Whereabouts was the *mavin*?" Will said it was beside the river. "It means margin, by my thinking, Will. You were wandering along the margin of the river." He sat forward, then, with his hands on his knees, as if to judge every word that he was offered. His eyes were bright and inquisitive.

"What then?" he kept asking. "What happened next?"

Will stumbled on, telling of the theft of the precious cart that had given Sim his tradesman's standing, and of that place that had seemed the best of all but then was cursed by misfortune; though that, his mother had said, would pass and the best would remain ... He told of Sim's staff that carried a piece of polished antler, carved with a whistle in its smaller tine, and how they had parted with it to their gaoler in order to get milk for Star. He told at last of the golden guinea that Delphi had found in that place where sometimes other coins had been found – only they were not gold.

"Coins?" Mr Hazelgrove cried. "What did you do with them?"

"Tossed 'em away, sir. They was thick wi' dry slubby."

This time Mr Hazelgrove laughed, though why he should do so could only puzzle Will. Anyone knew that slubby was much the same as stoach – and that came where cattle trampled wet ground into thick mud and puddles.

"Ah, Will," Mr Hazelgrove said. "We have much to teach one another of language. What a poor parson I have been to my people – I have not listened when they spoke strangely. I have even treated them as fools because I could not understand. And these slubby coins – do you know what I mean when I speak of the Romans – who were in this land once long ago – who left much behind them?"

Will shook his head. Did he mean Pharisees? Will

dared not ask for fear of seeming foolish.

"One day, Will, you shall take me to that place where you found the coins. Who knows what else we shall find? Such things delight great scholars."

The prospect of taking Mr Hazelgrove to that place pleased but still puzzled Will. What of the church-wardens – what of being put to work with some hard master who would beat the villainy out of him? In a stumbling way, he asked about this, his eyes on Mr Hazelgrove's face, watching its every expression.

"But there is no question, boy, of your being cared for by this parish – which is not yours. And where yours may be we know not."

"Then," Will said, beginning to tremble, "what come to me? Must I be shut in the prison?"

"No, no! God forbid! To be sure you shall work for your keep – but here. You shall not go till you run away – and that you must not do ... Now tell me how you all came to be together in the town gaol."

So then he must tell of Widow Tester, of the barn, of her marriage to John Penfold – and at the name Mr Hazelgrove looked both interested and startled. Why, if vagrancy was the charge, was not his father despatched to his parish, as the rest had been? Because of the goats, and because of the clothes, that belonged to Goody Nye, and she was dead and they were not truly hers ...

"One thing at a time, for mercy's sake!" cried Mr Hazelgrove. "No travelling man such as your father can live locked up – I have seen how they fare when this happens. More than that – it is my belief also that there is much spite at work in this business." He slapped his knees, stood up and began to walk up and down the room. "Tomorrow, Will, I shall ride to the town and seek out the justices' clerk, Robert Penfold. And we shall see what may come of that."

Could he mean that he would somehow gain freedom for Sim? Will dared not ask. Could such a man as Mr Hazelgrove, the rector of his parish, concern himself with a travelling tinker? Certainly he had shown much concern for that tinker's son – but did he know that Will and the rest had never been baptised? Once again, Will remembered the blind preacher and the wrath of God. Surely the wrath of Mr Hazelgrove could strike hard enough.

At this moment, the door opened and Mrs Hazelgrove came into the room. Without a glance at Will she crossed the room to where her husband stood on the hearth, his hands clasped behind his back.

"Forgive me for an uncharitable and hard-hearted woman," she said in a low voice. "Never let me fall behind you in my Christian duty. Let the boy have shelter here, if that is what you wish."

"There, my dear good Mary!" her husband cried. "I asked too much – too much. Dear generous soul, you must forgive me." He held her hand in both his, patted it and then kissed it. "Tomorrow," he told her, "I shall ride to the town and speak for the lad's father. Who knows, it may do good. I have some influence there, I believe."

"It would be a good thing," she agreed. "But I fear not tomorrow, Mr Hazelgrove. If you look from the window you will see that it has been snowing for the past hour and more. I doubt if any is likely to ride out of here tomorrow."

10

WITHIN an hour or two more the snow was piling against the house and the trees hung so heavy that all other habitation, the farm buildings, the church, had vanished. Peg and Dorothy sliding and shrieking, gathered in the roosting hens and settled them to lodge in the woodshed, whose door opened under the shelter of the kitchen porch. Leah's own pet hen, small and speckled, came into the kitchen and pecked about the floor for crumbs.

Released now by Mr Hazelgrove, Will sat on the edge of the settle and looked about him with more boldness than he had so far managed. He chewed at a great crust of bread that Leah had given him, first plastering it with dripping from a crock standing on the dresser. It tasted so wonderful that Will ate slowly for perhaps the first time in his life, munching and tasting and rolling each mouthful round his tongue. And all the time he watched Leah and the two maids pitching themselves against the strength of the weather and preparing for what morning might bring. They set brooms and shovels ready, laid sacks along the window sills and against the outer door, lest the snow edge its way inside. In the scullery, just beyond the first kitchen door, there was a pump drawing water straight from a spring. This was already wrapped and padded against frost, but now more coverings were piled upon it. As a further precaution, many buckets and crocks were filled and stood within the kitchen itself.

"The fire mun be kep' up," Leah said. She eyed

Will. "Here come your first task. Sleep by the fire – but see you wake times enough to keep it burning."

He nodded, half bemused by all the changes piling upon him as fast as the snow upon the rooftops – the clean clothes, the parlour, the warm kitchen with its three attendants; and now a bed by the fire. The little hen was already perched on the settle-back and Will would be glad to have her for a companion through the night. Of all those crowding so strangely into his life, the hen was the only one who was familar.

"Here, now – wrap up in that," Leah said, tossing Will a huge ancient coverlet that must once have graced the best bed in the house.

"My old cloak I come in," Will said, longing for it because it had been his own, "that'll do warm enough."

"That it will not – all that you come in got thrown out for burning – and naun too soon."

Will looked at his feet and was silent, for his eyes had filled with tears. He remembered how joyfully the clothes had been dragged from the chest in Goody Nye's cottage, how his mother had set aside those that were too ancient and wormy to hold together, and with what delight she had shared out the good. He put his hands over his face and pressed his fingers on his eyelids as if he would push back the tears. Where was she . . . ?

Now it was truly night time. The maids had gone to their bed in some chilly room under the roof, and Leah had vanished into her small closet next to the kitchen and pulled the door behind her. The house was so silent that Will thought he could hear the snow falling against the walls. Then the fire muttered, the ash fell as a log crumbled and he jumped up at once to tend it. The wood was dry and eager, the flames soon spurted gleefully. There was a pile of turves to one side of the hearth and he took three of these and placed them as he had often seen Sim do, when he wanted the fire hot and steady.

There was no bother in this for Will, for he had no desire or feeling for sleep. He lay down, but now he did not close his eyes. The warmth could not make him drowsy for he had too much to think about, too much to sadden him. He was bothered to know that there was still one thing he had not told Mr Hazelgrove. He had spoken of the goats, but he had not told how his lordship laid claim to them as his due, how in spite of that Sim had taken them for Star's sake. "They ran after," he told himself. "Whyn't they run t'other way?"

And worst of all his thoughts was the thought of Sim, lying in the bitter chill of the dank and dirty prison, his Queen of the Pharisees lost in the wintry countryside and her children scattered. And what if the snow stayed so long that Mr Hazelgrove forgot about riding to town?

Will stared up at the rafters and longed, as his father must be longing, for the stars. Yet he could not help knowing his own good fortune. A year ago, in the deep winter, they had dug themselves into the shelter of a brokendown bridge over a little reedy river. Snowfall had caught them unawares. As soon as the snow melted, they moved, but it caught them again before they found decent shelter. That was the worst cold of Will's life. If he listened now he still heard Fairlight's crying through the night, he remem-

bered Delphi's hands raw with broken chilblains and
his own sneezing that left his nose sore and red ...
The thought of all this seemed to increase the warmth
of Mr Hazelgrove's kitchen and at last Will slept. He
dreamt of finding the others and bringing them all
here to the warm kitchen, of Mr Hazelgrove smiling
at them, and his wife smiling, too. But when he woke,
with the dream still gripping him, he knew with a
piercing wisdom that he would never see his mother
in such a place as this. He knew that Fairlight would
be frightened out of her few poor wits, and that only
Delphi might pause and look around her and perhaps
nod her head.

When he slept again he thought he felt Delphi's
hand in his – then almost instantly, it seemed, he was
shaken awake.

"You must stir up and do a turn for your keep!"
cried Dorothy, standing shivering with no shoes on,
her hair all tousled and falling over her eyes. "There
you lie – snoring like some petted gentleman!"

Will flung himself from the settle, unwinding the
coverlet and tripping over it in his flurry. The little
hen, alarmed and angry, squawked and flapped, then
settled on his shoulder and pecked spitefully at his
ear. Will had hardly looked at Dorothy or at Peg, but
now he saw that Dorothy was a fat-faced, silly seeming girl, and her scream of derisive laughter hurt his
ears far more than the hen's pecking.

"Get to the pump fast, you grummert, and wash
your dirty face clean like a decent Christian. And see
you pull your shirt off'n you, or the mistress'll come
clucking. Washing wi' clothes on's no washing, so she
say. But mind all done's modest or she'll be at you

128

anyways!"

How would she know, Will wondered, since she was nowhere to be seen or heard. And what did modest mean? And where was the sense in pulling off his shirt simply to put it on again? He stumbled out to the pump and sure enough the water still ran in the dark cold morning. He slapped a little on his face and hands, since there was no one to see what he did or did not. And what was a "decent Christian"? It might be one with a clean face. More likely it was one whose birth was noted in those great books that Mr Hazelgrove had spoken of. It came to Will then, that although Mr Hazelgrove knew now that Will Swayne's birth or baptism was unrecorded in this church here at Sellingham, it might well not yet have occurred to him that it was recorded in no other. Then he remembered Widow Tester calling his mother's children "little heathens" and how she had scolded Moll for not taking them to church. He remembered, too, the blind preacher and remembered why he had spoken of the wrath of God. It was when he had told Sim he should have his children baptised and so avoid that wrath.

All this thinking and worrying was another new experience. Sim had decided for all of them and only Moll had ever questioned him. Now Will had to think for himself and his intelligence, put to fresh uses, was like some tiresome third hand or foot.

The first light was now at the windows and with it the strange snowlight, unlike any other. Outside there was already movement and noise, as Mr Hazelgrove's farm workers, his drover and his shepherd, his groom and his stableboy shovelled and brushed their way by lantern light to byre and shed and then to the kitchen for the first quick meal of the day.

"What's he?" the drover asked, setting down his lantern and jerking his head at Will.

"He's a whim o' the master's," Peg said, tossing Will a slight, fairly friendly smile. "He do have such whims, as well you know."

"Better this'n than last'n, I'd hope," the shepherd said, rubbing and slapping his hands. "Remember that poor sad waif we was all to pity – that ran off wi' the mistress's purse!"

The men began laughing. They eyed Will in a leery, knowing fashion, as if he had stolen a purse already and they would soon have it back.

"And then," Dorothy cried, "there was the poor little brother and sister that come begging, and was took in, and nex'dy was off wi' a great basket of meat and bread, and hidden under was two fine silver candlesticks I'd polished that very day – a pair of fine snuffers to match!"

"That come of a kind heart," said the shepherd, a woolly-bearded man, who now winked at Will in a manner more friendly than the rest. "The poor master niver do learn the cruel wickedness of others in this world."

Leah said, turning from the hob where she was stirring the pot and tasting its contents:

"Close your ears to 'em, Will. They'm a squacketting lot and don't pay for the hearing."

"Better a lad than a lass, surelye," the drover decided. "Keep 'un busy and there'll be no time for picking at the master's val'ables."

Will listened with little understanding. The only

thing he had seen since he came indoors that he would like for his own, was a fine sharp kitchen knife. What should be done with candlesticks – and what was a snuffer? Food was what he had stolen in the past, but food was handed to him here without question.

The men stood in a row and stared at him between gulps of ale.

"Make a good crowscarer, shouldn't wonder," said one. "Such'll be needed once the snow go over."

But the snow had only just started. It might last for weeks, and none would be able to venture far abroad. What if in that time Mr Hazelgrove indeed forgot his promise to ride to the town, or, if he remembered, might it be too late?

One by one the men wiped their mouths on the back of a beefy hand and left the kitchen. Each time the door was opened a bitter blast swept into the room. The house cow was lowing and calling from her stall, urgent for milking; there were two heifers besides, Leah said, and six over-wintering sheep that must be given fodder. Leah was clearing the table of platters and mugs and she paused to frown slightly at Will.

"We got you so clean and neat – what's to be done wi' you? You'd have scared the crows in them old rags, well and truly. But what now? There needs be better work for such a tidy-seeming lad."

If she was mocking, it was in a kindly way and by now he was able to know this. He looked down at his new clothes. He had slept in all but the jerkin but they still looked grand beyond words. He plucked stupidly at his sleeves, as if they imprisoned him.

"'I'd sooner the old," he muttered.

This time Leah laughed. She shoved a broom into his hands.

"Now sweep the floor and make it a good job or you'll get no dinner."

The threat was idle, and he knew it. He grinned at Leah, but in a rather puzzled way. He was not used to many others than his own family and each time he spoke or they spoke, he could not be certain what would be said or heard. The only broom he had ever held was a besom made by Moll or Delphi. This was five times the size, with great hard bristles such as he had never seen and a handle far too long for him. When he gave a firm stroke forward the broom almost carried him along with it.

Dorothy had come back into the kitchen and now stood watching him and shrieking with laughter. Leah sprinkled damp sawdust over the worn stone slabs and Will grew hot and breathless as he tried to sweep every speck from the cracks and cavities.

"Well enough," Leah said, "and shall be better next time. Stand the broom by the chimney corner. And pay no heed to Dorothy. The emptiest head makes the loudest laugh."

Peg appeared with an armful of clothes for washing.

"You must get at once to the master," she told Will.

Will looked at Leah as if for encouragement, for leave to go, and she nodded her head.

He hesitated. "Is it – the parlour?"

The word came out strangely and Peg mimicked him. "The parlyer – the parlyer? Whoever sat in a parlour, this time o' day. The master's wi' his books and his desk. The library is what that place is called, you ignorant mawkin."

"Let be," Leah said. "The door's on the left, Will. Cross the hall and you find it."

Will moved off warily. He stepped along the passage way from the kitchen, trying to keep his shoes silent, but being on the large side they slipped awkwardly, they seemed to clatter. Was this the hall he had come to? Which was left? The closeness of the walls, the several doors, the glimpse of a distant stairway confused him utterly. Why had he not run away fast when Mr Hazelgrove first rode by and seemed to rescue him? His appearance would have distracted Dan and then Will could have plunged off into the undergrowth that was thick and promising along that track. How much more comforting such surroundings would be than these, where every unfamiliar object threatened and alarmed. He was caught, he was trapped as surely as one of Sim's poor rabbits – he was as much in prison as his father was, and until the snow melted they could neither of them hope for escape.

Somewhere in the body of the house, women's voices could be heard in steady conversation. Will stood rooted and feared to move one way or the other. The women's voices ceased and now there was nothing but a regular tapping sound, as steady as a drum, that might almost have been his own heart's beat, had it not been so regular.

Then the sound changed. It grew to a great whirring and clanking and then to the sound of a hammer struck again and again upon the side of a bell ...

Will leapt in shock and fear, and flung himself

against the nearest door. It opened as he reached it and he fell through into the room beyond, his arm grabbed and held by Mr Hazelgrove.

"I am come to look for thee, Will. Was my message given? That you were sent for?"

"The bell frit me . . ."

"The bell? I heard no bell."

"You mun hear that'un," Will cried, hanging on to Mr Hazelgrove and looking back in dread. "Shall it clang again, master? Must I hear?"

"Lord, lord," murmured Mr Hazelgrove, shutting the door and urging Will further into the room. "He never heard a clock before! I forgot that my business is with a little savage. That is a timepiece, Will, that tells the hour to whoso will listen. Just now it struck nine times, you will recall." Then he paused and shook his head. "Nay – you may not recall. Can you count, Will Swayne? I think not."

Will answered a shade sullenly, for he was ashamed of his terror, "I know two hands mean ten fingers."

"And who instructed you – who told you that?"

Will did not answer. His mother had told him this simple trick, but he could not bring himself to speak of her. Instead he stood mum and still in another place that was full of strangeness. For here the walls held rows of books set orderly on shelves, while by the window Mr Hazelgrove's desk held much that he could not hope to understand. What was the curiously painted ball held within a metal arc – Mr Hazelgrove touched it with one finger as he moved to his desk and the ball spun magically. There stood, too, on the desk a handful of goosefeathers bunched in a small glass holder – these were more fitted to the mavin of a farmyard pond, in Will's opinion. He had, however, seen the clerk to the justices use such a quill for writing, so at least he knew what was happening when Mr Hazelgrove selected one, inspected its shaped tip and dipped it in a pot of ink.

"Come here, boy," he said, "and watch what I shall write."

By now, Will was so much confused that he moved like a log. He wished himself back in the kitchen where he need only sweep the floor.

"Look, now." Mr Hazelgrove said, pushing the paper towards Will. "What I have written here is your name. I have written *Will Swayne*. What do you think of that?" He looked earnestly at Will, as if expecting him to reply. As he did not, but only stared and stared at what was written, Mr Hazelgrove dipped his pen in the ink again. "There – there is my name below yours. *Samuel Richard Hazelgrove*. I make three words, Will, to your two – but it need not make me a better man."

Mr Hazelgrove's features were now becoming known to Will – the eyes more sad than merry, but so steady that Will knew they spelled safety.

"Now sit here in my chair," Mr Hazelgrove cried, growing eager in his teaching. "I shall hold your hand and you shall hold the pen and we will write your name together. Then perhaps tomorrow, you must write it for yourself."

Will put his hands behind his back. He could not know how desperate he sounded when he spoke:

"When'll snow be over? When'll 'ee ride about my father?"

Mr Hazelgrove sighed and laid down the pen.

"We are bound to accept what God sends us, Will. I shall pray the weather clears soon — soon. And see you pray, too." A sudden look of anxiety came into his face. "Nay — I shall pray for both of us until you learn how. Yes, yes — I know you have much to learn. But do not fear it. Do not fear the labour. Though God took my son from us, I see his purpose — I see it clearly. I shall teach you what I would have taught him. It will be harder for you — but one day, I can promise it, you shall have a place in the world above any a tinker's lad might hope for."

☆

THE SNOW lay high against the hedges and there was no coming and no going. The men had shovelled the yard clear for the sake of the beasts, but otherwise there was little clearance save a path from the house, through the graveyard to the church. There Mr Hazelgrove went on Sunday to perform his offices as rector of the parish. He took also his wife, certain of his servants, and Will. It was very cold. There were no more than six or eight parishioners attending the service, for most were snowed into their own holdings. Great clouds of steamy breath hung over every head. Mr Hazelgrove's voice, a different voice from the one he used at home, rang strangely in that ancient place, each word making its own echo. He had lost his smile and spoke sternly. The congregation shuffled its feet, perhaps in guilty shame at their way of life, perhaps just to keep those feet warm. Will thought of the blind preacher, with his roaring accusing voice that broke so readily into ringing, sturdy laughter.

Back in the kitchen, Leah and the rest stood close

by the fire and tried to thaw out the chill.

"The master pray loud for better weather," Leah said to Peg and Dorothy. "What journey was that he spoke on? Where'll he go, come the ways clear?"

Only Will knew. He felt greatly stirred that the parson had prayed loud in church for better weather – but would that come in time?

It was long before Mr Hazelgrove's prayer received its answer. Christmas came and went. Then the wind changed and a thaw set in. Soon it was raining, cleansing and scouring. The rain ceased and the wind blew strong and the ground began to dry. Men moved abroad even if not far from home. There was coming and going in the kitchen, villagers, both men and women, calling on business or to gossip. There was news of a death, news of two births, tales of disaster and of disaster averted ... The hens went back to their own place and Leah's speckled hen went with them. Wood had to be carted, logs to be split. Once, stepping with an armful of kindling over soft muddy ground, Will paused. He took a piece of wood no thicker than his little finger and bent down, and drew it in a vague shape over the ground at his feet. In his mind's eye he saw again the two wards Mr Hazelgrove had written and for a second he imagined himself able to write them here. But it was different and meaningless, and he stamped it out in angry disappointment ...

Next day the wind had dropped. The sky was clear. All that had dried then froze firm and promising. Another day the same and riding would be possible. The next morning, Mr Hazelgrove called for his horse.

137

"Who knows, Will. I may be in time. There may be some way."

Then he was gone. The day stretched eternally. There was nothing to prevent Will from running away now, for all was open. But he turned back to the house. As he did so, he saw Mistress Hazelgrove at an upper window. She was watching him. Perhaps she was hoping to see him run ...

Just at dusk, Leah went to the kitchen door and listened.

"Here come the master, now. I wonder he go so far for so little. He'd best have stopped over till termorrer."

Will shoved through the kitchen door, and now indeed he ran. He was at Mr Hazelgrove's stirrup before he had turned into the yard. Perhaps in some magical and mysterious way he had expected Sim himself ... But Mr Hazelgrove was alone.

"He'm dead a'ready!" Will cried out, gazing up at the rider.

"No, no. Not dead that we know of. But he broke from his prison, Will – that very night after you were all taken away."

"Where's he now? Where now?"

"He is gone – that must be your comfort. But a man unprotected through these last weeks of weather ... I fear for him. I do greatly fear for him."

11

"THINK, WILL," Mr Hazelgrove had said, as he sat by the parlour fire, weary from his ride, his dusty boots still on his feet. "Where might he go? If he still lives – and may it please God to have preserved him – where would he shelter? Think, boy – think."

Will had no need to think deeply. He knew where Sim would go if he had the strength and fortune to have beaten the weather. He remembered what his mother had said about that place – that the good would return and the bad be forgotten. When they left there after losing the cart, they had carried away less than half of what was stored underground. If Sim had found courage enough for the journey he might surely live there till the spring. It was a long way from the town where he had been in prison, and the days before that had not been easy; he would have been weak with hunger. Yet hard as it was to imagine a man travelling in such conditions, Sim Swayne was one who might have achieved the goal and be lying now sheltered and safe.

Stretched that night on the settle, the fire just glowing, Will tried to remember how to reach the place. There was more than one way which they had used, and each had been marked by Sim with knife cuts in the tree trunks. Once or twice, these had been cleaned and made clearer, remaining as a guide thereafter. One way that Sim had marked was the track that left the forest not far from the barn that had belonged to Widow Tester – Goody Penfold, as she had become. The second was far from there, towards the north where the land rose and the mound stood proud, the trees springing close and dense. That would be the way to take from where he now lay, Will decided; and the more he thought of this, the clearer he saw the track, and that place at its end, concealed and secret.

Moll had been right. He felt the good returning as that place welcomed the returning Sim, and gathered him to safety. He had only to go there himself, Will thought in the lonely night time, he had only to be re-united with his father and then it must follow that they would find the rest. They would be all together again. Moll would walk singing under birch and beech and oak. Delphi and Fairlight would stand shyly at kitchen doors and farmers' wives would give them eggs and crusts of good bread ...

Will's thoughts slipped into a dream and the dream took possession of him, filling him with wild ideas. He had no need to stay here in this place of strangers, however kind. This was a life he had watched and now knew a little, but it was not the life he had known, it was not his life ... He turned uneasily, telling himself again, and then again – this was not his life.

He rose to mend the fire and the warmth met him and embraced him. It was very dark, the darkest of the night and the fire was the only waking eye in the place. In the body of the silent house Mr Hazelgrove's fine clock struck some hour that Will could not yet count – though he got halfway.

The sound roused him as he crouched on the hearth. He rose and moved lightly about the kitchen. On the dresser was a loaf resting on a board and a knife beside it. Crumbs had scattered on the floor beneath and as Will approached a couple of mice scurried away. He cut a chunk of the bread and then went to the larder. There was meat there, and again he used the knife, slicing from a ham and a joint of roaster beef. He tied the meat and the bread in a cloth that hung with others near the fire and stuck the knife through his belt. Then he took the big coverlet that Leah had given him for his bed, folding it in four; he wrapped it round him for a cloak, and it was good and warm instantly, in some way comforting him for what he was doing, even though he had chosen to do it. His shoes, that were a shade too big, he carried to the door, setting them down while he drew the bolt. It rattled, but anyone waking would think only that the fire was being mended.

The door opened easily, too much in use to betray him with creaks and squeaks. He pulled it behind him and felt at once the bitter air, striking at his face and head, at his hands and feet that were no longer accustomed to living out of doors. It was frosty and clear, there were stars and a blazing bright slice of old moon just setting. These gave him his direction; he turned north-east by the church, seeing as he did so that the dark would not much longer keep the stars so sharp and glittering. A dog barked and another far away. As he stepped out on to the track, he saw a fox slinking on a low belly along the hedgerow, and gave it a whistle, as if claiming a fellow conspirator. The fox turned its head, checked for a second in curiosity, then loped unhurrying on its way, as if recognising in Will only another night-time creature.

Will's breath clouded and almost crystallised, the

air was so chill. He watched the fox away and then began to hurry. The movement warmed him. Though his eyes smarted with the cold, his body began to glow and tingle. He broke from a trot into a run, snatching off his cap, his hair blowing back from his forehead and his ears, leaving his face naked. He opened his mouth to the clear air and gulped in freedom. With every leaping stride his spirits rose until he began almost to caper along the deserted way. Soon he would recover all he loved. Soon all problems would be resolved. They would be together again.

Now the first light wiped away the stars, though the moon still kept its radiance. By the shape of the ground ahead Will could see that he was moving in the right direction, for the forest swept over great hilly banks, carrying with it hordes of still trees, an army frozen on the march.

Then, as if the loss of darkness showed him what he was doing, Will thought of the waking house left behind him. He thought of Mr Hazelgrove, of how they would go to him and say, "That boy, master, that you sheltered – that boy has gone the way of all the rest." He stood still, appalled – not that he had run away to find what he had lost, but that he had done so without thought of what he owed. Mr Hazelgrove had saved him, had tried to save his father. Mr Hazelgrove had fed him daily, kept him warm, spoken on his behalf to a resentful wife, given him clothes. Though Will understood only a little of it, he was aware that Mr Hazelgrove knew well his foundling was an unbaptised heathen and therefore, by the thinking of any churchman, unworthy to live alongside Christian souls.

And there was something more – something so strange that he hardly knew which way up to hold the thought. It was to do with writing his name – with books that were stuffed with unspoken words to which Mr Hazelgrove held the key. He remembered how he had tried to write in the mud with a stick, and he looked around him wildly. There was a stick almost at his feet with hard by it a puddle, the frost thick almost as snow.

The light was growing. He crouched down and tried again to remember the shape of what Mr Hazelgrove had shown him. As if by doing so he might somehow make his own ingratitude seem less. About him now, as he took the stick in his hand, came the sounds of day beginning. Dogs barked and cattle stirred in their byres, lowing to be milked. Above Will's head a late owl drifted home and beside him on a bough glittering with hoar frost, a robin burst into violent song.

The stick moved in his hand like a dowser's hazel twig. He muttered, "Will – Will –" as though by speaking his name he would see it magically forming in the puddle's frost-furred surface.

As he spoke in this way to himself, he remembered his mother crying out in a frenzied, crazy way to the clerk a word that sounded partly like his own name. Will – Willow – Will ... "Where were you baptised? Which church? You shall remember the name of the church ..." and Moll, frantic, had cried, "St Wildered!" "St Wilfred," he had corrected her.

St Wilfred! That was the place. There had been a village name, too, but that he found impossible to drag up out of his memory of that awful day.

Will leapt to his feet. He ran. Somewhere not too far away — for the cart that carried them from the town had been ordered back by nightfall — there was a village whose church was the church of St Wilfred. He would not find there what he was seeking, he could not hope to find his father in such a place — but he would find his mother, Moll Swayne the Queen of the Pharisees.

So, when he came to the track that led eventually to the forest, he turned aside, keeping to the road that ran for many miles from village to village.

☆

THAT was a long day but it was fine and crisp. Will had not much food with him, so he managed to eat nothing until noon. After the first excitement, he had been sobered by the distance between villages, by the long lonely tramp, hardly a soul about, the weather being so cold. By mid afternoon he had seen only two churches and neither was named for St Wilfred. At one he asked an ancient man walking by what the church was called; at the other he found gravediggers at work, battling glumly with the bitter hard ground. They answered him shortly, staring, but Will could not tell why.

When dark returned, Will was no nearer the end of his search, and now he was filled with self-reproach. He should not have allowed himself to be distracted by the remembered name. Had he continued as he intended he might now be within reach of reunion with his father. This, however, was not quite the truth — or not all of it. The truth was that one quest was as uncertain as the other — the truth was that he should never have run away without a word to Mr Hazelgrove, who had defended him and cared for him.

His spirits low, his heart empty, Will wrapped himself up in his makeshift cloak and settled into a dry ditch under a well-kept hedge. He ate the rest of his food, trying not to wonder where the next might come from, lay down and waited for sleep. The cold grew sharper, the ground harder. He remembered the warmth of the parsonage kitchen and seemed to hear all those voices telling Mr Hazelgrove that he had once again been betrayed ... He slept at last and dreamt, then woke not knowing what the dream had been except that it had left tears almost freezing on his cheeks.

At first light, Will dragged himself out of the ditch and went stiff and hungry on his way.

☆

"What do you lack?" the woman asked, standing at the barely-opened door and looking at Will in a hard, shrewd way.

"A bit o' bread, mistus, an' a sup o' water – and any task you need doing to pay for'n. Yard cleaning – or wood chopping – or crow scaring."

"Crow scarers mostly look like scarecrows," she replied. "You're a sight too tidy for such work – and none such needed till sowing time, you silly lad."

Will had forgotten about his clothes. He should have known better than to ask for work out of season.

The woman was already closing the door.

"There's other sorts I can do –"

The door opened again, this time a little wider.

"You shall have your sup o' water," she said. "I'm as much a Christian as the next." She pushed the door but still kept an eye on him as he drank. "Now be off," she said, though not so sourly as he might have expected.

Defeated, he turned away. He tried to walk upright, but his stomach would not let him and she must have seen his state and felt some pity for it, for the door opened again.

"Wait there till I cut you a slice."

Will leant against the door jamb and waited as she had told him. He heard the woman moving about inside, making a slight clatter, and heard her speaking to someone unseen. She was grumbling about the nuisance of beggars forever at the door.

"Now – get on your way and fast about it. And thank the dear Lord you knocked on a door that come soft in the middle."

Again the door was closing. Again he spoke and she paused.

"Is there a church hereabouts – named St Wilfred . . .?"

"If any ever think of it in these heathen times, the church here is named for St John – that was Jesus Christ's most loved disciple. Say your prayers there and feel the better of it." She peered at him. "Are you a papist?"

He said no, very quickly, since she clearly suggested it could be the worse for him if he were. He knew the name, but not its meaning.

"It's papists pray to saints," she said, and closed the door sharply and finally, he even heard bolts rattling home.

Will walked away. He saw the church almost immediately, set on a mound, squat, with a low tower topped by a very small spire. He went slowly and wearily and sat down on a tombtop and opened the bundle of food. She had parted with all but half a good loaf, a hunk of meat, some cheese and a slice of bacon pudding. Sitting there in the graveyard he could just see the farmhouse chimneys. There was enough food to keep him for two days and he wished he had sounded more grateful.

The sun shone thinly and now there seemed no one beside Will Swayne in all the world. The church itself, that gave some shelter from the wind, was very old and weary, bedded down hard into the ground that had held it for centuries. The door stood open, hanging on only one of its big iron hinges. Had he known any more prayers that he had picked up almost surreptitiously from Mr Hazelgrove, Will would not have been tempted to offer them in that neglected place. He ate carefully and moved off.

Now the road twisted interminably and it was without any habitation. The forest on which he had turned his back was still to be seen behind him, black against the winter sky, in no way inviting. But he knew it better than he knew these unpromising lanes.

The next time Will came to a church it was down a hill instead of topping it. Its door was shut and three or four sheep were cropping the graveyard grass. Next to it stood the parsonage, a far smaller house than Mr Hazelgrove's, though it was made of the same stone and had a garden with a fine yew hedge and a tidy pathway to the door. Making a rough triangle with these two buildings was the farm, its house modest, its barn enormous. There was movement about the place, men still working outside, hurrying as dusk touched the sky to grey. Within the house as he moved nearer, crouching and peering by the low wall that separated consecrated ground from the hurly-burly and dirt of the farmyard, he heard the voices of women, and their laughter. A light shone in a downstairs window. Then a door opened and a girl came out with a bowl of scraps for the fowl, which instantly rushed squawking towards her from every corner of the yard.

Will watched the girl as she coaxed the birds towards the fowl house, laughing out loud as they shoved and pecked. She was young, her hair neatly tucked under a white cap, and she was entirely taken up with the matter in hand. Watching her, Will put his hand against his chest, his heart was thumping so fiercely. He opened his mouth to shout, but his voice resisted him, he could not order it into shouts and cries. He stood in a dream unable to shake himself awake – for in the dream the girl was Delphi.

Then she turned on her way back to the house, the hen house door securely bolted behind her.

She moved towards him. She wore a dress of plain brown, almost smothered by an apron too big for her. She walked firmly and easily. She appeared to be at home.

"Delphi . . . ?"

But it was only a whisper and she did not hear. He scrambled over the wall and ran towards her, and the movement made her turn. His voice came to him, then, for he was sure.

"Delphi! Delphi!?"

She started, looking for a moment as if she would take to her heels. Then she hesitated. Then she knew him.

"Willow!"

She ran to meet him. They stood hugging and laughing, not knowing what to say to one another, barely understanding what had happened.

"Quick!" he said at last. "Is there food you c'n bring? Fetch it, then. We mun go fast from here."

"Will . . .? Go fast?" She looked bewildered.

"Wake up! The master broke from prison and did run. He'll be at that place, surelye. We mun go to him, I say!"

"Go to him? You and me?"

"How otherly?" He stared at her, not understanding. "Find our mam first, then," he said, "and take her wi' us. St Wilfred's. I got back the name – the church name that man writ down. You know what I'm saying. Don't stand so mum."

She pulled away. "I remembered the name, too. She went from there."

"'You don't know that!"

"I do. When the churchwardens sent me here, I did cry and bawl for mam, and Farmer Appleby – he went to find her. But she'd bin and gone."

"Where'd she gone?"

"None could tell."

Will stared at her. He saw that she had changed a great deal. Not only was she clean and tidy but she had grown plump. She looked easy, content.

"You're never Delphi – you're never my sister Delphi. She talk another way."

"And you look another way!" she said, sharply.

"Who gave you such clothes?"

"I'll tell come we're on the way."

"No, Willow – no. It's winter. Snow'll come again. Where'd we shelter?"

"Winter's bin often, long afore now."

"It's warm here," she said, looking at the ground. "The kitchen's warm. The fire burn like summer. There's meat on the spit. I sleep in a bed wi' Milly and Sal."

"Who's Milly? Who's Sal?"

"Sal was a foundling. Milly's the mistus's poor relation."

"Where's Fairlight, then?" he demanded, alarmed.

Delphi screwed her hands together and looked away. He knew she did not want to remember.

"Where's Fairlight? What come to our sister?"

"Speak soft, you grummert – mistus'll hear." She looked at him, biting her lip, shaking her head. She spoke in a voice so low he barely heard it. "Fairlight did die. You'll not see poor Fairlight again, Willow." Now at least she sounded more like the sister he had known. She put her hands over her face and began to cry.

"Oh Delphi – what come to her? Here? Were it here she died?"

"Before here. Another place. It was a bad place and Fairlight got set on to caring for the geese, and the great gander flew at her and pecked and hit wi' his great wings. There was frost on the pond side and she slipped and fell in. She fell into the pond, Willow. There was no more'n a handsdepth of water – but she banged her head and never got up . . ."

"She drowned? Fairlight?"

"Aye. She drowned as she lay ... There was none near but a little lad five year old."

Will said stupidly, shaking his head, refusing to believe, "It were Star died – not Fairlight."

"Both."

He stood thinking about her, a wild skinny creature without any more wits than a sparrow and just as easily dead ...

Someone called across the yard, a woman who stood at the open house door.

"Where are you gone, Philadelphia? Come in from the cold, child." It was a kind orderly voice and Delphi turned at once.

Will grabbed her hand. He saw the time going and knew that if he lost Delphi now he would lose her for ever.

"Come wi' me! Come wi' me!"

"Leave go!"

Delphi's voice was sharp. She jerked her hand away and was gone, calling as she went to the woman at the door.

"Who's that with you out there?" Will heard the woman ask, rather stern.

And he heard Delphi answer, "My brother, ma'am."

The woman called something, but Will had turned and was running back through the churchyard.

The dusk now gathered. The sky had changed and there was a light wind. He went fast down the roadway, casting off the village and glad to be alone. When the true dark came he had difficulty in finding shelter for the wind sneaked in everywhere. At last he came to a rickyard set well away from its farm, and

151

there was the remains of a hay rick there, fallen over the ground so that he was able to creep in and pull the hay over him for a cover. He ate some of the food that was left to him, then tried to sleep. He thought of Fairlight, but he thought more of Delphi. He thought of their mother who was none knew where. He woke in the dark and his face was wet, as if once again he had been crying in his sleep. But it was snowing and the flakes had melted on his cheeks. He got up at once and stamped some warmth into his feet and swung his arms. He huddled his cloak around him and began again to travel. Only now he was retracing his steps.

☆

THE SNOW came and went in showers blown on the wind, so soft it was difficult to recognise an enemy. The lanes and tracks that had seemed so long as he went from Mr Hazelgrove's kitchen were surely longer now. He could not get warm as he had been able to do in the excitement of setting out; and his heart and his thoughts were colder even than his shrinking body. He hated and cursed himself for having changed his purpose after setting out, he hated and cursed himself for creeping back the way he had come. Would he ever see his father again? Was his mother as dead and lost to him as Star and Fairlight – and as Delphi? Was he the only one left of the Queen of the Pharisees' children?

And then came the bitterest thought of all – that he was as changed as Delphi and could not ever be the same again.

That night, after a day's tramping, the snow began to fall faster. The flakes were swept and spiralled along the ground ahead of him. The snow melted and then froze, then fell again. Will slipped and stumbled. He had a little food left but he felt no need of it, he had no time to pause and eat. The snow began to fall fast, as though its course had been decided. Great swooping laden clouds shed their load over all the land, falling and settling on Will's head and shoulders, creeping after a time through the good wool cloth and lying damply against his skin. How many times had this happened in the past and he had thought nothing of it and it had never harmed him. Who was he to blame Delphi? Soft and snug, like her, he had given away his endurance.

The snow made its own light and later it stopped for a time. The surface froze, making going easier. That last sliver of moon appeared, and Will paused to take off his shoes and empty them. An hour later, very lame, he came by the squat old church with its hanging door, and this time he went inside. Two or three stone steps led up from the nave into the chancel, and the fell against them and huddled there till morning. No one came near except mice and a rat or two busy about their own concerns, and small birds flying, as soon as it was light, in and out of the open door. By the time he set out again he had lost count of how long he had been on the way. There was nothing for it but to trudge on, and it was something that he had little fear of losing his way, since any side tracks were on more than paths leading into woodland. He saw no one, for all were busy about making their own homes secure against the weather.

The snow started and stopped, started and stopped. Sometimes there was a burst of sunlight, but not enough to dry Will's clothes. He was unable to speed up his progress, but went snudging on his way like a weary old man who is no longer certain what he is thinking.

Now it was dark again and the snow came faster. Will fell down several times and at last it was forced into his mind that he must hurry or die by the roadside. He managed to move a little faster, and then his shoes, heavy with wet, fell off and rolled away. He was left in his stockings, and in one way this made progress easier.

He knew the parsonage immediately it loomed through the dark and the weather, by the way it lay at an angle to the road, which curved away beyond it and disappeared. There was a light in one window and Will was urged by it into a last effort that helped him almost into a run. He reached the kitchen door and fell against it. He fell so hard that Leah came running at once, as if answering a summons.

Leah cried out to someone behind her in the kitchen, "Come quick and see! It's Will Swayne at the door. Lord – he do look that pathery and strange!" She caught his shoulder crying, "Wicked lad! Wicked, wicked, ungrateful lad! There's naun for thy sort here!"

Someone said, "Wait, Leah – wait!"

It was not Mr Hazelgrove's voice, but his wife's. She put a firm hand under Will's chin, turning his face towards her. He could just see in the dimness that the mistress of the house was crouching beside him, but he could not see what good or ill was in her face.

"Go quickly, Leah," she said. "Fetch the master. And send Peg and Dorothy here fast. The boy's in sore need." And as Leah went back indoors, Mrs Hazelgrove took Will's hands and began to rub them, trying to warm them into some sort of life. "There," she said, "you did well to trust this house. You are home now, poor child. You are safe."

12

"ADAM AND EVE," said Mr Hazelgrove, "did eat of the fruit of the Tree of Knowledge. And so, my poor Will, have you. But let us not forget that the world as we know it grew out of that deed in Eden – and just so a world shall grow for you."

Will had no idea what this meant. Even if he had not been dazed still by the meeting with Delphi and the struggles that followed it – not only in his snow battered body but in his thoughts – he could still not have understood. It was to please Mr Hazelgrove that he looked so attentive. And Mr Hazelgrove was indeed pleased, for he smiled and nodded.

"Let you be a patient pupil, Will, and I shall be a patient master."

Even this simple statement left Will fumbling for understanding. He knew only that he was safe, that he was forgiven, that his return had excused his flight. Like Delphi, unlike poor Fairlight, he had found a haven – though in gaining it he had lost much. When he was carried indoors half frozen to death, he had been put to bed in one of the many small closets in the upper part of the house. When he recovered, the place remained his. It was not so warm as the kitchen, but fortunate in being in part alongside the chimney as it soared up the side of the house. He was alone there, and he had never been alone before. There he lay awake long hours and wept wildly for Sim and Moll, for Fairlight and Star, for Delphi and for himself.

When Will wept for himself, he seemed to weep for

a stranger. He was no longer his known self but a different, old boy, befriended and cared for yet parted from all he had loved. He would never live again as he had once lived. Like a fox cub orphaned, like a deer's lost fawn or an injured bird taken indoors and taught to live there, he had lost his kinship with the wild.

☆

THE SNOW stayed long in those early months of the year, as often it will when the first fall comes before Christmas. When it cleared, March had come and at once the spring stirred and struggled.

"Now, Will Swayne," Mr Hazelgrove said, "you must come with me to the church, for my conscience cannot support your soul's danger any more."

Will was by then accustomed to agreeing with Mr Hazelgrove and to making mighty efforts to understand him. He followed him into the church, where they were quite alone. Mr Hazelgrove first knelt and prayed, and Will knelt by him rather awkwardly. Then the parson went to the font and, there being no vessel available at that moment, he took the water in his cupped hands.

"Bow your head, boy."

Will did as he was told and tried not to hop and squeal when the water was tossed over his head, while Mr Hazelgrove prayed loudly and fervently.

"Now I am your sponsor in the sight of God, Will, and shall care for you as for a son. Say after me, *I believe*!

"I believe," said Will, gazing on his benefactor. His belief was in Mr Hazelgrove himself, not in his mysterious God, but it seemed enough for the present.

One evening, after Mr Hazelgrove had been away about his own business all day, Will was called to the parlour. There was Mr Hazelgrove busy with his mulled ale, while on the far side of the hearth his wife sat with her sewing. She looked up at Will and smiled, eyeing him up and down.

"The jerkin fits well," she said; and no more, returning at once to her stitching.

"Aye," agreed Mr Hazelgrove. He glanced at his wife in a pleased way, for the jerkin, of course, had come from the store of his dead son's clothes, and it had been that son's mother who had given it to Will. "You look a well-set-up lad. Your health is restored. You shall prosper."

He finished his ale and set down the pot and then said slowly and carefully, "I fear, Will, I have news of your father that shall pain you. And of your mother, too. Since I have said that I *fear* I have news – you will know what it must be."

"No, sir," said Will, sick with dread.

"A man has been found dead on the forest fringes – as, alas, happens too often in winter. There was a woman with him."

"There's lots dies o' the wintertime," Will muttered, looking at his feet, sullen and full of fury. "You said it."

"These two were found by an honest fellow, Will. In the man's pocket he found a guinea – and did not keep it, but handed it to his employer."

"There's a lot o' guineas, surelye ..."

Mr Hazelgrove broke in, urging him to accept his loss. Had not Will himself told of the coin, and how it could not be spent for fear it should seem stolen?

"She —" Will began. He was silent a second and then changed what he had been going to say. "She find'm, then. She run through the winter and find'm."

"They were together," Mr Hazelgrove said, looking down at his hands and wondering, perhaps, things being as they were, whether they had any right to be so. "Well," he said, "however it be, may God rest them."

His wife said quietly, without looking up, "Amen to that, my dear."

"You must bow to God's will, " Mr Hazelgrove said. "At such times, Will, as I think you begin to understand, there is no other help for us but to accept his wisdom."

"Aye, sir," said Will, though he was still puzzled.

"You have a home here, so long as you care to keep it," Mr Hazelgrove was saying. "And so long as you are an industrious and willing pupil. Is that not what we have decided between us, Mrs Hazelgrove?"

And again she said, without looking up, but in a kind accepting voice that Will would never have hoped to hear, "Amen to that, my dear."

"Go now, then, Will," Mr Hazelgrove said. "It is late. Get to your bed."

Will went to his own place and lay on the narrow bed and thought about the golden guinea. He thought how Moll had paid it for a favour never granted. Some other man, then, lay dead with a guinea in his pocket.

☆

JUST as some traveller in distant parts may find an untamed savage and bring him home to be civilised, so Mr Hazelgrove set about instructing Will. It was a hard and often bitter business for both of them. Often enough Mr Hazelgrove's promised patience broke into red-faced fury, often enough Will scowled and resisted. But it was bound to be the master who won and the pupil who submitted – if only because the pupil's curiosity got the better of him. On a day in early summer, Mr Hazelgrove came a little late to the day's lessons in the library. He found Will with a book in his hands. He had pulled it from among the rest on the shelf and now held it gingerly.

"What do you find there, Will?"

"I – am," said Will – and then looked up grinning. "You taught that! *I am*!

"There now," Mr Hazelgrove said. He put his hand on Will's shoulder. "At last we have made our beginning."

Deep down, Will knew that he was finally trapped, but he knew, too, that his resistance was over. Now he accepted all he was offered, striving hard and long to please his master. He had gained much and would not think of his lost freedom. He shut his mind to the past and would not think of what he had been, how he had lived, what he had loved. Only his dreams remained invaded. When he slept he heard again his mother's strange cry of farewell as the cart carried her away. She had known, he told himself. She had seen all that was to come.

☆

A LITTLE short of summer's ending, Mr Hazelgrove's sister, Mrs Godley, came visiting with her husband, her daughter, Arbella, and her son, James. They lived some miles to the north, only a little way from London. James Godley was the first genteely reared boy that Will had encountered and he could not like what he found. Arbella, about Will's own age, was not beautiful like Delphi; she looked at him with curiosity, but after a time, she smiled. The sounds in the house changed. There was fresh movement and laughter, less time for lessons as Mr Hazelgrove and Mr Godley enjoyed one another's company. The two ladies constantly chattered. Though the visitors interrupted Will's new life, sending him back to spend time in the kitchen with the servants, Mr Hazelgrove was pleased to show off his pupil as opportunity offered.

In the kitchen, the mood was less kindly.

"Back where 'ee belong," said Dorothy. "What come of dinner wi' the master and mistress, eh Will? Did 'ee spit bones over the cloth like a tinker's lad?"

"Let be," said Leah, as usual. But most of her warmth was gone. She looked at Will with reserve, careful in her talk and checking the rest if they spoke of the master – as though there was a spy at the table.

About the seventh or so day of the Godleys' visit, Will was called to the parlour after supper. There they all sat – the ladies together by the open window, Mr Hazelgrove straddling the hearth, Mr Godley, a large gentleman, sitting near with his hands comfortably clasped over his stomach. Young James sat fidgeting on a hard chair, while his sister struggled with the business of netting a purse, frowning and concentrated.

A few months ago, Will would have fled in terror from this well-mannered arangement of gentlefolk. He managed to bow, as he had been taught, but he could not stop his feet from shuffling as he stood waiting to be spoken to.

"Tell Mr Godley, Will, of that forest place – where you found coins lying. The dark, dirty coins – the slubby coins," he added, smiling. "Tell Mr Godley what you know of all that."

Will could not start. The mention of that place sent his heart into his mouth. He felt almost faint as he struggled for words.

"There was – there were many," he said at last.

"They found these coins, Henry," Mr Hazelgrove said to his brother-in-law, "and seeing no use in them, tossed them away. This must interest you, I supposed." And in his kindliest manner he explained to Will, "Mr Godley is much taken up with ancient matters. He is a learned member of a body in London – made up of such scholars as he. He will tell you all about how the Romans conquered this land. He is forever in search of what they left behind them when they went away."

"If it were them left the money, sir," said Will, no longer able to sort out *were* and *was*, "then they left more. Great timbers come from a dwelling – and, sir, a hole underground – a great chamber –"

By now Mr Godley was thoroughly roused. He sat forward on his chair and put his hands on his knees as though he might at any moment spring to his feet, in spite of his bulk, and set out at once to see what Will had described.

"A chamber underground ... Coins ... Great timbers lying ..." He turned to his host in much excitement. "Does his lordship know of this? He is, after all, a patron of our society – and the land must be his own ... Have you had communication with him over this?"

"No indeed! I move in less exalted circles than you, brother Henry! I would not presume to send him word except over parish matters – tithes, and churchwardens' meetings and so on. But if indeed you consider this a matter of interest –"

"Of more than interest – of importance. Is the place so far that we may not ride there and back in a day? The boy knows the place. He shall be our guide."

Will stood stunned and silent. The thought of going again to that place filled him at once with dread and longing. The longing was to see what he had once loved, perhaps even to find some sign that Sim and his mother lived or had died. The dread was a different matter altogether. This lordship they spoke of could only be that lord of the manor whose due on the death of Goody Nye should have been the goats that Sim had lured away – that Robert Penfold had falsely claimed as his own. Did high and mighty men remember such matters? If so, might Sim's son have to pay for his father's offence?

Now Mr Godley was on his feet and striding about the room while his wife sighed at his unmannerly energy and complained to Mrs Hazelgrove that there was never a moment's peace now that her husband had become an antiquary and cared for nothing better than he cared for ancient history."

"Believe me, my dear sister – his wife and his

children are nothing – nothing! He loves only some great battered stone that he may take in his hand and pretend it is a thousand years old!"

Mr Hazelgrove very quickly became infected with his brother-in-law's enthusiasm. All else was forgotten as they planned and plotted, each crying at moments in the rapid conversation, "The boy shall tell us that." Or, "Will knows what is there and shall show us. Will shall lead the way."

The days being still long and the light lasting, it was agreed that at the next full moon, if the weather were suitable, they would set out at sunrise and hope to return by midnight.

13

THAT morning began the tenth day of a spell of fine weather; the sun for that time had banished all blue from the sky, leaving it flat and infinite. And when the sun came up that morning it was plain that the weather would not break today. The parsonage was quit too early for either loving wife or lazy son or shy daughter to wave farewell – but looking back to the house Will saw Arbella Godley standing at an open window. She looked deserted and even at a distance, resentful. For a second he saw how irksome life might be for the only daughter of even the most modest gentleman. He remembered Delphi – Delphi as he had known her, not as she was now. She had come from a world Arbella could never enter, about which she probably knew nothing and would learn of with a shudder ... Arbella must have seen Will turn, for very slightly she lifted her hand ...

Mr Hazelgrove rode his sturdy old grey, and Will sat a shade uneasily the pony he had lately been taught to use. Mr Godley had come visiting with his own horses and rode a chestnut, a carriage horse that was none the less an easy ride. Accompanying them on one of the farm horses was Marty, who worked as a stable lad at the parsonage; he carried a basket packed by Leah with chicken and bread and a bottle of wine, all covered neatly with a cloth.

As they rode out, Mr Godley was already thinking in a big voice of how, if the place indeed offered what Will promised, the news should go to his lordship of the manor.

"He must of course be informed and give permission before our searches can proceed. I would there had been opportunity to suggest he be with us today." And he looked in a satisfied way at his brother-in-law, who must surely be impressed by these high connections.

Will rode in silence. A keen sense of terrible betrayal gnawed at what Mr Hazelgrove had recently explained was his conscience, the voice of his soul. Why had he brought these strangers to a place so full of recollection. He should have come here alone, never with any other. Had he done so, he felt now, he might have found what the voices and movements of strangers must surely drive into hiding. For he could not rid himself of the conviction that Sim and Moll still moved about the forest, that he must come face to face with them and know the tale of their death to be false ... And then there crept in another thought that he tried to defeat but could not. He remembered Delphi – so changed that for a moment or two he had not recognised her. He, too, was changed – perhaps even more than his sister. What if he in his turn should have become a stranger?

Until they reached the edge of the forest, Will stayed dumb and tormented. There he led them off the well-worn wider track and they moved into the shade of tall beeches whose branches here and there were just touched with the promise of autumn.

"The little track," he said then, veering to his left, aware of them all following him obediently.

Now they rode in single file among young birch trees little more than ten or twelve measures high. They ducked under low branches and now must thread their way. The young trees grew in clumps of five and six, where the seeds from parent birches much older had blown and scattered, yet stayed close enough to prove their kinship.

Mr Hazelgrove called out to Will, "Are you certain of the way? It is extremely tortuous. What if we lose ourselves in this density?"

"We must trust the guide, sir," Mr Godley rebuked him.

Ahead, the way opened suddenly, fanning into a clearing. Here Will found what he was looking for, an oak with a cross carved in its trunk. Sim's knife had made that cut and it was almost as if his hand still rested there. The talk between the gentlemen had shaken Will a little, but now he knew he had chosen well. Increasingly the forest took on its remembered twists and turns, its sounds of running water and birdsong; its thousand secret eyes seemed to Will to be watching his return. He had never seen the place from horseback before, but its shapes were imprinted somewhere behind his eyes and no rise or fall in the ground was unfamiliar; he expected a landmark before he saw it. Coming from this direction they must pass the iron-working that lay steeply above its ponds. Away, far away to the south-east, was the old burnt house, with Goody Nye's cottage a mile or so along the bottom ...

As all this swelled into his memory, Will tried to count the time since he had last known the forest. A whole lifetime, surely, had passed since then, changing all that he had been and had known, filling him with new sense and knowledge. It was, for all that, only a little over a year since he had watched his mother dancing in the fairy ring with new-born Star in her arms. That meant he had come into the next year of his life without making it – the willows had been barely in leaf, she had often told him, when he was born down by the river. He had inches more height now as well as being able to read some hundred or so words, and to write his own name whenever he chose. His manner was different and his tone of voice. He was no longer the strange creature he must have seemed to Mr Hazelgrove at the beginning. With each admission of alteration in himself he saw how unchanged was all that spread around him. His eye sharpened to its old powers and he thought he saw a thousand birds, coloured or dun, shifting and flirting among the branches. There darted the scutty-wren and there the pink, the caffincher – looking high as they moved across a clearing, he saw a hovering kestrel, making ready to stoop. A pheasant's call almost brought him the smell of stewing, rising from a simmering pot. A rabbit dashed and his hand went halfway to his belt, where his catapult had hung. Passing under a tree tangled up with wild woodbine, he snatched a piece still flowering and stuck it in his cap ...

As he did so, he glanced round at Mr Hazelgrove and saw him very slightly frown. Will thought, "He fear I go ..." and it was not vanity that made him think so, but a newer instinct that prodded him with a reminder of promises and obligations, of bargains struck and of the books in the parsonage library ... "He fears I may go," he corrected himself ...

By noon they had come to the first river that slit the bottom some miles below that place. It was very hot and still.

"We'll bait here," Mr Godley decided, before Mr Hazelgrove had time to speak. "There's water for the horses and a fair little stretch of good grass. Now then, Will Swayne, are you an honest guide – do you lead us where we should go?"

For a second Will was tempted. He might lose himself and all of them and be blamed for it and not care greatly about that. If he did so, he knew he might never get to that place again, for he would not be asked to act as guide a second time. He must go on. He was dragged forward by his own dread and longing. He could not go from the forest without first knowing if that place stayed silent and unpeopled, without looking into the underground chamber where the food store had been made – without knowing if Sim had indeed wintered there, wherever he might be now. He would never rest until he knew certainly that there was no one there whom he remembered.

"Aye, sir," he said. "This is the way, surelye."

"How much further, then, boy? We are already very far from home."

"Two-three mile. No more."

☆

THAT place was very quiet. Not silent, for a breeze shifted lazily through the trees and a thrush, a missel thrush, loudly assertive, sang somewhere high up among the far beeches. The sun was now journeying fast through late afternoon. There before him stood the great yews, their trunks mossed over with that close leafage that had seemed once like the green bodice Moll had rescued from a village bonfire. The ground stepped back before Will, as if inviting him forward, as if bowing him to that place. It seemed bigger than he remembered. There was no sign of a fire, no sign of any man having paused here on whatever journey. But had that man been Sim Swayne, Will knew that the appearance of the place would be the same.

He had heeled his pony up the bank ahead of the rest, and they had paused – as if waiting for him, their leader, to order them on. And he kept them waiting, dreading their intrusion, dreading what certainty must come when he led them to the underground chamber and they all peered in.

He dismounted and tethered the pony. He went back to the head of the deer-run up which he had ridden to the summit.

"Here! 'Tis here, masters. The place is here."

Mr Godley, in a state of considerable excitement and agitation, came up fast. He flung himself out of his saddle and tossed the bridle to Will. He began at once to stride about, to pace and to measure. Then he came to the timbers, all but a few now broken stumps, the rest lying scattered and rotted about the ground.

Mr Hazelgrove had followed his brother-in-law more sedately. He, too, dismounted, calling to Marty to take his horse.

"And take my brother's, also. Will – we shall need you."

He went at once to join Mr Godley. Will handed the bridles to Marty, who grinned at him and said in a manner not altogether unfriendly, "Do as he tell, young Master Will!"

"Will!" Mr Hazelgrove called.

"Come here, Will, and hurry!" cried Mr Godley.

He went to them at once, his mind thick with memories – of hunger and the greedy snatching at food as they sat round the fire, of watching Sim working away at the antler, of listening to Moll singing, of sleeping under the stars and waking at first light bitterly hungry again ...

"Where is the chamber you mentioned?" Mr Godley asked. "The underground chamber. Here where the timbers lie? Is it hard to open?"

There was a great mound of cut bracken over the entry, but it was brown and dry and could have been last year's. Will began tearing at it, tossing it away, wresting it from the brambles that had threaded it all together and now mauled his hands painfully – but he was glad of it, for it punished him for his treachery in bringing strangers here. It could never be the same again and he was the one who had brought on what must surely be its destruction.

The last of the covering was dragged away. He saw the ring set in the stone slab that sealed the compartment and seized it. He had never raised it himself till now, and would not have been able to when last he was here. His strength had doubled in a year. The slab lifted and was laid back. The chamber was exposed to view, the sun slanting in neatly and displaying it from side to side.

It was empty. No stores remained. Someone had come and gone. Will knew it could only have been his father.

☆

'WE SHALL return another day," Mr Godley said. "We can proceed nowhere without his lordship's sanction. He will be greatly interested – greatly. I believe we are about to learn much of the past." He put his arm across Will's shoulder and gave him a firm, approving pressure. "You have done well. Do you know, Will Swayne, that when this is written of, your name may well be set down along with the illustrious rest?"

Will did not answer. He looked at the ground and thought about the goats. But he did so briefly, for his newly growing shrewdness told him that he need have little to fear from the Lord of the Manor now. He frowned, struggling to understand matters that were far beyond him. With only half his mind he heard the gentleman nabbling on about these Romans, how they had come here, what they had done here – about the iron smelting and about fortifications, and other such learned confusions. Mr Godley gauged where the sun might strike at midday – which Will could have told him and saved him his strenuous calculations; Mr Hazelgrove murmured about religious significance, and apologised for knowing so much less of the whole business than his learned brother-in-law.

Now it was time to go. The horses had been fed and watered and all was done that could be done for that day. The light had turned rich and golden, the birds were in tumult, their throats might almost burst with the fervour of their singing. It was a place to stay in, not to leave – it was a place where the whole world might change, where mystery hummed like a great swarm of bees. The scent and the sound of magic had hung over all the days of Will's life and he heard in and smelled it now. He dragged behind as the rest moved off, Mr Godley in a state of the highest excitement allowable to a man of his sort. Will tugged at his pony, holding back, lagging, lagging far behind, dreading to leave, dreading to miss the promise that spread so subtly over all that he could see about him. It was the time of homecoming. It was the time of day when travellers sought their rest, moving over well-worn paths to well-remembered resting places.

He heard Mr Hazelgrove call. "Will! We are leaving you behind!"

In desperation, Will snatched off his cap and hurled it away among the undergrowth. He spurred his pony down the bank carelessly and stupidly. Then shouting to Mr Hazelgrove when they were all but level, "I left my cap!" he swung the reluctant pony's head and went back the way he had come. Again he heard Mr Hazelgrove calling after him, "Hurry! We cannot wait for ever!"

The firm, commanding voice, that Will had learnt so greatly to respect, struck at him oddly. He almost turned ... But there was too much at stake – he was too certain of what would come. He gritted his teeth and dug in his heels, forcing the angry pony up the bank. Once again he tethered the creature. He began to run fast from spot to spot circling what was already a circle, running in that magical direction that Moll called widdershins, against the sun – as though in doing so he summoned unnamed powers to his aid. On the western-most side, where perhaps, Mr Godley had said, there might be the remains of some fortification, the sun now struck so low that it dazzled him.

From here, if he shielded his eyes, he could look

towards that far track they had so often travelled, and so often at this time of day, coming by the iron furnace and the great ponds, coming that last time, with Star already ailing and trouble they could not guess at lying just ahead. As plain as if she stood beside him, he heard his mother singing.

He went down quickly, even shyly, on one knee, and laid his hands flat on the remembered, the re-membering ground. Ahead of him there was some movement under the beeches, a cart and horse approaching slowly, a man at the horse's head ... A charcoal burner maybe ...

Will told himself this because he dared not admit his belief that the man was Sim. He knew him but would not know him, dreading disappointment, the fading of the dream as the light changed, the shadows shifted. But then he saw that a little behind the cart a woman walked and he could almost certainly hear her singing.

He leapt up. He flung his arms wide and went hurtling down the bankside towards the beechwood, calling as he went, calling to his father and to the Queen of the Pharisees.

☆

SIM checked the horse. He stood staring at Will. Saying nothing, waiting. Moll moved to his side, curious, peering at the stranger.

Then she said, "Who's come, Sim?"

Will caught her about the shoulders, felt her resist, and drew back to look at her.

"'Tis Willow!" he said. "'Tis Willow, surelye. 'Tis Will Swayne – your son! Mam!" He just prevented

174

himself from seizing her again and shaking her. His voice changed. "Know me!" he said. "Know me . . ."

She turned away, saying to Sim, "Better you speak wi' him, husband. He talk so crazed – see you send him off."

Sim took Will by the arm and led him a little way, while Moll took the horse's head and frowned after them, her song quite ended.

"Ah, Willow," Sim said, his voice very low and gentle. "For all the finery I do see and know thee well . . ."

"What come to her, master? What come to her wits?"

"Leave 'un, boy. I'll tell soon enough. Leave 'un till I say." He held out his arms and Will went to him, discovering for the first time as they embraced, how much he had grown, for his cheek was now level with Sim's.

"Now tell, master. Tell all you may." Again he said, anguished, "What come to her? Tell! Tell!"

"More'n she could bear come to her, Will. Sorrow and starving – and the prison walls."

"But she see me a stranger!"

"More'n she might bear, I said. She put it by and forget. And best so. When I find her first – when she run here from where they took her and I run here from gaol – she seem all but dead. Then we go fast into that place together, and the snow kep' us and there was food. She came to herself, but it was what I first knew of her – and all else lost. There was naun in her life but Sim Swayne. Willow was gone, and Delphi, like Fairlight and Star ... Come spring I were at the furnace and earned the cart and horse of a fellow

175

that got sick and mun' die."

"I should've stayed by you, master! I should've yelled and beat about so they shut me up close wi' you!"

"N'more'n a child then. And now you change. I see you prosper."

"Aye," Will said, ashamed of it. He thrust Sim aside, crying, "I'll speak wi' her! I'll see she remember!" But Sim pulled him back. "Let me go, master!"

"Let be," Sim said in a low voice. "Let her rest. Maybe — one day ... But not yet — she best not remember yet. And I'd sooner it were niver."

Now Moll called out. "Time to go, Sim. Let'un be off. Sun's down. We'm late enough."

She was smiling, easy. Her wits were there, and her merriment. Only her memory had gone, had been set aside. Waiting a shade impatiently, she fondled the horse, stroking and patting, chirruping to the creature, then singing under her breath.

"Where will you go?" Will asked. "Where, master? Shall it be that place?"

"The old house. There's good keep and grass enough for the mare." He put his hand on Will's arm. "There's naun for grieving over. All's well wi' us!" And he shook Will's arm, saying again, "All's well! All's well wi' us!"

"Come, Sim, come!" she called.

"Wait, my lady," said Sim.

He went to the cart and fetched something from it, then returned to Will. He was carrying the staff with the carved head of deer horn.

"Take 'un," he said, thrusting it into Will's hand. "I snatched it from 'm — that prison devil — beat him about the head so he fell ... Take 'un and forget the rest. She forget – and it bring her to be happy again."

Then he went back once more to Moll and took the bridle and the horse moved off, the cart on the rough track jolting and clattering its load of such remembered objects as broken pots and iron nails, as wooden clothes pegs and birth brooms and various other symbols of a tinker's trade.

They turned off on to the track that would lead them to the old burnt house. Will stood watching them. Neither turned. One hand on the bridle, Sim's other arm was round Moll's waist. She leant against him, walking with the swing and ease of a girl, her face upturned to him so long that he stooped to kiss her. The last sun sent spears through the trees, and the cart, and the two of them, moved in and out, in and out until Will's eyes dazzled and he could see no more. He waited and waited, but they did not reappear where he had expected, so they must have cut onto that track that was little more than a deer run but led faster to their resting place.

He ran up to the top of the bank, still hoping to see them once again, for the land cleared a little ahead. The wind had frisked into a chilly breath, another hint of autumn, blowing too soon over the last of summer. Will moved back slowly to his impatient pony. As he went he thought again that he heard singing. He soothed the pony and led him down the bank.

As he reached the lower ground and prepared to mount, he saw Mr Hazelgrove waiting at the head of their homeward track. How soon had he turned back – how long had he been watching there and how much had he understood ...?

"I feared you had left us, Will," he said, answering a part of the question. "I thought you might turn back with them to your old life."

Will stood staring at the ground.

"So both are living after all, Will. I am glad."

Will looked at him quickly, only just raising his head.

"She forget all – she forget me and all on us. My father tell me that's best."

"I believe him to be a wise man."

"Sir," said Will, forcing out the words, "ought I go to 'un?"

"Ought you to go to them?" Mr Hazelgrove repeated, corrected. "You must do what you know to be right. There is no harder task. Go after them, if you think best."

"They'm gone. It's too late ..."

"Yes, Will," Mr Hazelgrove said. "I think it is." He waited a second as if expecting Will to speak, but he was silent. "Come then, Will Swayne. We'll not reach home tomorrow at this rate." He eyed the staff in Will's hand. "That is a fine thing your father gave you. It must help you remember what your mother has been helped to forget." He smiled slightly and touched Will's arm. "Put all your trust in the Almighty. He shall make all well."

☆

WILL hauled himself up into the saddle then, and at last they moved off. He felt weary and yawned as he rode. He rode carrying the staff like a lance, and the wind, now so much freshening, blew through the antler and sang gently. It sang to him, as it would for ever, in the high strange magic voice of the Queen of the Pharisees.

THROUGH THE DOLLS' HOUSE DOOR

Jane Gardam

Claire and Mary love the dolls' house and its curious assortment of residents: the outsize Dutch doll, Miss Bossy; the General and his troop of Trojan soldiers; the miserable Small Cry; the mysterious Sigger . . . But little do the girls know of the extraordinary lives and adventures, past and present, of this resourceful band and the marvellous stories they have to tell.

"An original story . . . wry and funny, and full of a sharply poignant sense of the passage of time."
Jill Paton Walsh, Books For Keeps

THE SWORD AND THE DREAM TRILOGY

Janice Elliott

The King Awakes (book one)
The Empty Throne (book two)

Outcast from the City with his mother and baby sister, young Red finds a Britain devastated by a nuclear holocaust and inhabited by savage tribes: Outmen, cannibals, Magickers and War Lords. Pursued by the evil Guardians, Red's one hope of survival lies with a mysterious stranger – a soldier called Arthur, woken from the distant past to fulfil a famous legend...

"A most inventive fantasy of a future world."
The Times Literary Supplement

"An exciting tale of quest and pursuit."
The Listener

SOMETHING RARE AND SPECIAL

Judy Allen

Following her parents' divorce, Lyn has to move out of London with her mother to a temporary home on the coast. At first, missing her old friends and city life, Lyn feels like a fish out of water in this bleak, empty land-scape, but then she discovers Bill Walker and his binoculars – and something very special ...

This is a beautifully written and atmospheric story by the winner of the 1988 Whitbread Children's Book Award.

"A sensitive story, rich with thoughtful atmosphere."
Junior Education

EVACUEE

Gabriel Alington

Young Fanny Clegg is evacuated to America to escape the wartime blitz of London – while her brother Hugh joins the Royal Navy. Sent to stay with her "Aunt" Bird, Fanny finds herself in an unsettling world of sophistication and luxury. Bird's daughter Pepper seems friendly enough, but her son Jay is openly hostile. And, as Fanny soon discovers, he is not the only one.

"Many girls will identify ardently with Fanny in her trials."
Geoffrey Trease, TES

THE HORN OF MORTAL DANGER

Lawrence Leonard

When Jen and her brother Widgie stumble across a secret underground world, they find themselves in the middle of a war between two rival factions, the Railwaymen and Canal Folk. It is the start of a thrilling and dangerous adventure.

"A fantasy whose words are forcefully visual, whose concept is original and compelling."
Growing Point

"A lively original and exciting adventure story."
The Times Literary Supplement

STRAY

A N Wilson

Unanimously acclaimed as "a classic", A N Wilson's *Stray* is the wonderfully imaginative life story of an alley-cat: a tale of adventure, romance and terrible inhumanity...

"A N Wilson has written a classic in the sense that Black Beauty is a classic... His episodic, quasi-picaresque story is deeply read-on, funny, moving and exciting."
Brigid Brophy, The Literary Review

"A must for moggy maniacs."
The Daily Mail

"A cat of literary distinction, and worth meeting."
Naomi Lewis, The Observer

ANANCY-SPIDERMAN

James Berry

Anancy, the hero of these twenty lively and intriguing Afro-Caribbean folk tales, is both man and spider. Seemingly defenceless, he is an artful rogue who uses his cunning to outwit his opponents – the mighty Bro Tiger in particular. But these are just two in a colourful cast of characters which includes Bro Dog, Bro Monkey, Old Higue Dry-Skull, Swing-Swing Janey and many, many more.

"James Berry retells these vivid stories . . . in a soft, mellifluous voice that captures the magic and trickery of the spider hero."
Julia Eccleshare, Children's Books of the Year

VAMPIRE MASTER

Virginia Ironside

There's something very sinister about Burlap Hall's new biology master, Mr A. Culard. He hates light, loves bats and eats dead flies! Now the other teachers are starting to behave oddly too. The question is: will young Tom and his friends, Susan and Miles, manage to get their teeth into the problem before it gets its teeth into them?

"A very funny novel which keeps up a steady pace of entertainment and suspense."
The Bookseller

"Entertaining . . . Hilarious moments."
Junior Bookshelf